The Hunt for The Hades Manifesto

Millenium Pursuit

By Theo Douglas

Table of Contents

Chapter One: The Forgotten Relic

There were long shadows cast across the maze of trenches and partially excavated items by the Grecian sun's harsh brilliance as it colored the site in a dusty gold shade. It was easy to decipher that the sharp contrast of contemporary tools against the background of deteriorating ruins was humanity's never-ending curiosity about its past stories and adventures.

Carter had mastered the art with years of practice and effort. His hands were crafted with precision from years of practice. He had only a portion of the tales buried that were beneath the Earth— stories of battles, love, betrayal, and long-gone civilizations. The designs that came to the surface from the ceramic fragments after he tirelessly removed layers of ancient dirt clearly depicted a time of art and culture in the ancient metropolis.

The students and some of the experienced archaeologists worked together on their task. The air was filled with the rhythmic noises of brushes, shovels, and whispered talks. However, at that very moment, Carter's universe shrunk to the objects he had in his hands and their historical implication.

He paused a moment to think about the potter who might have created this object, the hands that held it in the past, and the events it had experienced for centuries. The shard was more than just a piece of history; it was a silent reminder of how quickly time had gone by.

While contemplating and considering all that had happened in the ancient world, Carter's seasoned eyes noticed another object partially buried close to the pottery shard. He wondered what it was. This item would push the limits of myth and truth. As he was ready to peel back more of the layers of the past, his pulse increased, giving him a rush of eagerness.

The area of the excavation was a bit chaotic, but in an effective way. It would have appeared hectic to an outsider: archaeologists giving instructions, students eagerly taking notes, and local laborers directing wheelbarrows to do their job. But beneath it all was a choreographed dance in which everyone understood their place. There was an apparent camaraderie and a real hunger to learn more about the past, and everyone embraced that fact Carter was heavily preoccupied with his recent discovery as he stood far from the action. The ceramic shard was safely packed and tagged next to him, but he paid close attention to the partially hidden stone. His careful excavation sparked interest among the nearby archaeologists and students.

The first one to approach him was Rhea Papadopoulos, a young Greek archaeologist with brilliant eyes, raven-black hair, and brimming enthusiasm.

"Dr. Williams? Are you okay? You seem distracted." She hesitantly spoke.

He raised an eyebrow, temporarily startled by her observation.

"Oh, Rhea," he managed to say with a grin. "One doesn't come across anything that feels so strangely familiar but out of place every day."

Her interest grew, and she looked at the newly appearing artifact. "May I?"

Carter nodded and smiled, admiring her attention to detail. The anticipation in the air increased as Rhea leaned in, and they both sensed this discovery might be much more significant than any typical find. As Carter continued to remove soil and debris from the stone, his mind immediately returned to the long-forgotten myths, the buried secret discussions, and the undiscovered Hades Manifesto.

Carter and Rhea's skillful fingers carefully continued to remove the soil from the stone tablet. Although it was small, its importance was substantial. Even though the writing on the tablet had aged, it was still possible to read what was written. Carter noticed the geometric patterns and the graceful, curved lines but paid more attention to the symbols. These differed from the regionally usual glyphs or scripts that one might anticipate. Some of them reminded Carter of symbols he discovered in unclear academic writings, symbols connected to the Hades Manifesto. This term had been the subject of many late-night discussions, but he had always attributed it to mythology.

Half out of excitement and half out of worry, he felt a shudder down his spine. The aura around the object seemed to be vibrating with its vitality. It was strange.

Sensing the seriousness of the finding, Rhea said in a voice barely above a whisper. "Do you know these symbols, Dr. Williams?"

"These symbols are associated with a legend or myth that has been disputed and debunked for decades, despite my conviction that they are true." Carter struggled with the right words.

Unwavering in her stare, Rhea met Carter's. "Perhaps, just perhaps, some myths are based on reality? It could be possible."

Carter and Rhea continued to look at the iPad, their surroundings seeming to blur in the background. Each mark, etching, and symbol told a story that had existed since the beginning of time, contradicting their beliefs, and understanding. As the team's whispers and murmurs became louder, more attention was focused on the discovery.

Always the scholar, Rhea reached for her notebook and drew the symbols quickly while speaking to herself in Greek. Her fingers ran across the pages as she compared the symbols to the ancient alphabets, she had already studied a lot of times.

Carter's mind was racing with several ideas. He could recollect passionate discussions with instructors, late-night chats with Alice, and even the skepticism of colleagues when the Hades Manifesto was brought up as a topic. Considering that this item might be the precise thing about which those legends were written was thrilling.

Carter was abruptly awakened from his daydream when a mighty hand touched his shoulder. It was renowned Greek archaeologist Dr. Dimitris Karas who served as the group's local authority. Dimitris was a respected figure on the dig with a graying beard and tired eyes.

He asked solemnly, "Carter, what have you discovered?"

Carter realized that the archaeological community would soon feel the impact of their discovery. He had no idea how the tangible reality and the mythical world were connected.

Dimitris leaned down and scanned the writing on the tablet with a blank gaze. Everyone appeared to temporarily stop talking around them as they became acutely aware of the seasoned archaeologist's assessment.

After what seemed like a long time, Dimitris finally stood up straight and rubbed his chin in thought. "I've seen many relics in my time, countless writings and symbols, but this... this is something else." he said mysteriously.

Carter found his voice after swallowing. "Um, Dimitris, I know it sounds a bit unbelievable, but the symbols fit some of the descriptions from the old myths. It's connected to the Hades Manifesto, you know."

Dimitris responded to Carter with a focused stare, "The Hades Manifesto is more than a story; it's a contested chapter in our history that many have sought, and some have died trying to find. You step in dangerous waters, my friend."

"But Dr. Karas, consider the possibilities: If this is indeed related to the Manifesto, we might be on the verge of rewriting history," Rhea said, expressing her youthful vigor.

Dimitris agreed with her observation by nodding. Then, he continued solemnly, "We might be opening Pandora's box; some things are hidden for a purpose."

The seriousness of his statement lingered, leaving the assembled crew with questions and a lot of doubts.

The excavation site, which was once a hive of excited activity, had evolved into an amphitheater of quiet conversations and side-by-side glances. The atmosphere was heavy and dense even though the afternoon sun had produced a dappled pattern on the ground due to the weight of the old stone.

Elara, a renowned linguist from the University of Athens, muttered as she joined the group, "Dr. Karas has a point, I believe." She was well-known for decoding scripts that had stumped even the most seasoned archaeologists, all due to her aptitude for ancient languages. The earthy tones of the place stood in stark contrast to her blazing red hair.

"The wrong kind of attention could be harmful, so we must act with the utmost prudence if this is connected to the Manifesto." She spoke.

Carter delicately touched the stone with his fingers and said, "We're discussing potential risks in the present and historical ramifications. Am I correct?"

Carter was staring into Dimitris's eyes. "Legends describe the Manifesto as a key to secret knowledge and power, which can tip the scales of the universe," Carter said.

Rhea turned to look at them, her determination visible in her eyes. "Then, we must take steps to keep it safe, but first, we must unlock all of the mysteries."

There was an affirmative nod. A trip that wobbled between myth and reality had begun, filled with unexpected dangers and opportunities as well.

The team assembled in a temporary tent to review findings and make plans for the day's work as the sun sank and painted the sky orange and purple. The area around a large wooden table was now free to accommodate the tablet. It was lit by a lot of dimly lit overhead lamps, which caused the walls to throw long, creepy shadows.

Taking over, Dimitris laid out several ancient parchments and scrolls next to the tablet.

He said, "I guess for many years, these have been nothing more than amusing bedtime stories or academic curiosities, but now... they are some of the oldest recordings and rumors about the Hades Manifesto."

"They might serve as our guide, you know." Carter piped in.

Elara started tracing the characters with a fine brush while recording her interpretation; her command of language was obvious. "Greek is present, of course, but there are also Coptic, Aramaic, and other elements that I have yet to identify in the script." She said on the recorder.

Rhea was overly excited, "We're studying a Rosetta Stone of legends from the past! Wow!"

Carter's thoughts went quickly to Alice Moreau. Their time together at the university was distinguished by their shared love of mystery and enigma.

"We'll need additional knowledge; I am aware of someone who can assist," Carter said.

Dimitris confirmed the statement and added, "We're traveling through unfamiliar territory, so every piece of information will serve as our compass."

Carter sat outside the tent later that night, a satellite phone cradled in his hands beneath a blanket of starry skies. The chirping of crickets in the background was audible in the distance, periodically broken up by the gentle rustle of greenery. He hesitated because their finding was still weighing on his thoughts. Calling Alice's number wasn't only about enlisting her assistance and encouraging her to join in on a risky hunt.

He dialed the call button and waited. "Dr. Moreau speaking," said a recognizable voice.

"It's Carter. The team has found something... unparalleled," he said, trying to hide the urgency in his voice.

There was silence. "Carter, you sound serious. What is it? What have you discovered?"

Carter inhaled deeply. "I know it's a lot to take in, but we need your expertise," said Carter. "It might be a section of the Hades Manifesto."

Another pause, but this one was longer. Then, Alice responded, "Send me whatever you have. I'll catch the next flight," in an excited tone.

A rush of relief swept over Carter, and he sighed. They would have a capable comrade on their voyage and a great archaeologist with Alice on board. The puzzle pieces were gradually fitting together in a bigger picture.

The following morning, the camp was active with activity as daylight broke. Workers and archaeologists worked together to prepare for another day of digging, mapping, and labeling. Despite being carefully buried behind layers of cloth and placed within a safe case; the tablet continued to attract everyone's attention in the camp.

Rhea was studying a sizable map across a table as she was already immersed in her job. Rhea attempted to connect the possible origins of the tablet based on the languages that Elara had discovered using the map's depiction of historic trade routes.

Dimitris approached Carter in the meantime with a worried look on his face. "We might require more security, glancing at the guarded tent where the tablet was kept. If news gets out about our find, there's no telling who might come looking for it, you know," he said.

Carter nodded and continued, "I'll make a few calls. I have contacts from my military days."

A car's noise abruptly broke the peacetime of the early morning. A vehicle drove into the campsite, and a dust cloud formed in advance as if to signal its approach. Dr. Alice Moreau had come, as shown by the tall woman who emerged with her blonde hair pulled back and a sense of determination in her gaze.

Carter smiled as he approached his old friend, knowing the adventure had just begun.

The camp was immediately thrilled by Alice's arrival, which was like a breath of fresh air. She walked with assurance, scanning the area before turning to look at Carter. Her face was a mix of friendliness and curiosity. The friendship between Alice and Carter was evident as they hugged, bearing witness to their mutually shared history.

With a humorous undertone, she said, "Carter, you're constantly digging up trouble, huh?"

He chuckled, "And you, Alice, could never resist a good mystery."

After the initial greetings, Alice's attention switched, and she said, "Show me your discovery. I am interested in it."

Carter and Dimitris took Alice to the tent and showed her the tablet. Her eyes grew wider as she observed it. She traced the engravings with awe and remarked, "It's beautiful, isn't it?"

"And harmful," Dimitris said.

Alice raised an eyebrow and looked at Carter, "Can you explain that?"

Carter and Dimitris presented their research, theories, and the impact of the Hades Manifesto over the following hour. Alice began to put the pieces together in her critical mind as she analyzed the information.

She said, "We're on the verge of something momentous, and we need to move quickly."

Due to Alice's presence and her dedication to their cause, the team had a strengthened sense of purpose. They all felt connected with each other.

Later that afternoon, the group gathered beneath a canopy to take cover from the glaring heat. Laptops, magnifying glasses, brushes, and other archaeological gear were set up at a temporary workstation. Alice pulled out some notes she had written during her travel about various texts and papers she had read over the years that might shed light on their current mess.

Alice said aloud, "Legends of the Hades Manifesto have been whispered through the corridors of academia for years, but most regarded it a mere myth. We're one of many to take this route."

Elara said, "The linguistic fusion here shows some attempts, like almost as though cultures joined for this," as she tried to understand a section of the tablet.

"Or they were all attempting to protect or manage its influence," Carter ranted.

The group fell silent as the topic of power was brought up. They all realized they might be holding the secret to a weapon of unfathomable power rather than just an antique artifact.

Looking at Alice and Carter for guidance, Rhea asked, "What's our next step?"

After giving it some thought, Alice said decisively, "First, we decipher. Knowledge is currently our best protection."

The camp became a center of passionate activity as the days passed on. Alice and Elara were habitually absorbed in old books, cross-referencing every little nuance. The team's relationships were characterized by enthusiastic disagreements, frustrating periods, and random epiphanies.

Carter took a minute one evening to survey the camp from a distance, the soft glow of the lamps illuminating the continuous activity. With a flask of coffee in hand, Dimitris approached him. He sipped and said, "It is great, isn't it? History may change due to us,"

Carter nodded, focusing intensely on the lit tent where Alice worked hard. "Dimitris, it's not just about the past; whatever we find could have important repercussions for our present."

Rhea had discovered something strange within the tent. She told Alice, "Look at this pattern; it doesn't seem random; it reminds me of star constellations."

With her heart beating faster, Alice leaned in closer. She said, realizing the possible significance, "You could be onto something. Something pretty big."

The tablet was more than simply a store of outdated information; it may have served as a map or a guide. Its mystery proceeded to reveal new layers of untouched information. The knowledge of the celestial constellations refreshed their passion for their profession and made it more urgent. Alice took over since she was intensely fascinated with astral patterns from her previous study days. They set up a projector to compare the patterns carved onto the tablet with contemporary star maps.

The group gathered outside the tent under the starry sky. The projection of the ancient pattern and the stars began as Rhea pointed the projector at a white sheet. The team's awe boomed when the patterns overlapped.

The first to say, "Okay, I think it seems as though these constellations are suggesting some specific places on Earth," was Elara.

"Astral navigation. That's what it is. Ancients were experts at it. They might be leading us toward the next piece of this puzzle," Alice said as she looked at the stars overhead.

Carter located the potential spots on his satellite map as he pulled it out. He thought their next stop would be in the center of Africa if they were correct in their interpretation.

"It would make sense for something as ancient and potent as the Hades Manifesto to originate there," Dimitris responded, "The cradle of humanity."

The dangers in the shadows were getting closer, even though their path was becoming more evident with time. The crew's dynamics started quietly changing as preparations began for the trip to Africa. There was a bit of stress and excitement about the next journey. Carter took on the role of the tactician, planning the safest routes, procuring supplies, and ensuring communication lines were secured. He did this by drawing on his military experience. It was easy for him.

Alice was occupied in the study. One night, as the party huddled around a campfire, she muttered, "There are stories of an old city hidden in the African plains, a site where the skies meet the Earth."

"A city of stars?" Elara wanted to know.

Alice said, "Legends claim it was a sanctuary where old wisdom was protected."

"Legends also mention the guardians of the area. They won't take well to outsiders." Rhea said.

"Every treasure has a dragon, but with the appropriate approach, dragons may become allies," Carter continued, poking at the fire.

"Let's hope they are like archaeologists," Dimitris chuckled, constantly trying to lighten the mood.

None of them could avoid the weight of duty as laughter resonated through the night. They were going into an area where legends might come true. Dangerous legends.

There was a frenzy of activity at dawn. Vehicles were loaded, supplies were double- and triple-checked, and equipment adjustments were made right before departure. Carter arrived with a little metal case and walked to Alice as daylight reached the camp.

He pulled out a satellite phone and said, "I've been storing this for emergencies. If things get out of hand, we use this direct line to some former contacts from Delta Force."

Alice turned to face him and spoke, "We should hope that we won't have to."

Elara and Rhea were busy making sure the old tablet was safely packed. The importance of ensuring its safety could not be stressed enough.

"Next destination, the heart of Africa! Lovely, isn't it?" said Dimitris as the engines roared to life.

The dig site that provided them with the first clue in this complex puzzle was left behind as the caravan of vehicles set out on its trek. A route with unknown obstacles, ancient mysteries, and uncertainties lay before them. However, the group was motivated by a goal more significant than themselves.

Chapter Two: Into the Heartland

The diverse African environment, with its vast savannas, dense jungles, and mystery plateaus, reflected golden in the early morning sun. The engine's humming sound was almost hypnotic and relaxing. Alice and Carter flew toward their destination in a small, chartered plane. They saw it as the start of a trip that would change history, even though it was just another region of the planet to anyone with an inexperienced eye.

With a book open on her lap and packed with drawings and notes about the star city mythology, Alice rested back in her chair and sighed. Every element that she studied for days added to the mystery surrounding their search mission. Alice peered out the window and observed that isolated pockets of civilization had lost way to the grandeur of the African wilds. She felt a surge of anticipation growing inside her.

Carter sat across from her, his eyes rigidly fixed on what lay ahead of him. He had been to Africa on multiple assignments before and was familiar with the territory, but this trip was unique. All it had was only old mythology, and the prospect of discovery existed; mission orders existed, thankfully.

For a split second, their eyes connected, expressing enthusiasm, firmness, and the seriousness of their shared goal. Both were aware that they were about to go on board a meaningful journey and that Africa was waiting for them with a lot of surprises that may be dangerous.

The influence of the plane's tires on the uneven tarmac broke the pair's silence. The heat and aroma of Africa welcomed them as they arrived in port, a blending of parched dirt, wild flora, and the distant smell of wood smoke. They were at the start of their adventure at Kigoma, which was a city in western Tanzania.

Carter instantly took control of the situation and signaled a passing porter to assist with their stuff. He turned to her and spoke in a confident voice, "Alice, I've set up a meet-up with one of my old contacts from my Delta Force days. He's familiar with the area and has some connections that could prove useful."

She adjusted her hat while giving a nod. "I'll just focus on learning more about the Star City tale, you know since we need to be sure we're going in the right direction."

A tall man with a friendly smile walked over to them. His deep-set eyes, covered with traditional attire, showed signs of experience and wisdom. He hugged Carter and said, "Dr. Williams, it's been so long. And what a lovely surprise, I must say."

Carter returned the greeting and introduced the man to Alice. "This is James Mwamba. Welcome to the expedition, and this is Dr. Alice Moreau," James said.

James shook Alice's hand firmly. After greetings and introductions, the group started through Kigoma's busy streets, searching for the next puzzle piece. "Welcome to Kigoma, Dr. Moreau. I've heard a lot about you. Good stuff."

The neighborhood market in Kigoma was a kaleidoscope of hues, sounds, and scents. The streets were lined with stalls offering fruits, clothing, and handicrafts as hawkers screamed about their goods.

16

Sharp shadows were formed by the midday sun as individuals went about their daily activities.

James led the way as they made their way around the market, giving many familiar individuals hearty handshakes and engaging in playful conversation. He was well-liked and respected in this town.

Alice decided to stop at stalls decorated with hand-carved objects and beautiful beadwork and ask about local mythology and stories. She questioned a vendor, an elderly woman with silver braided hair, "Can you tell me the importance of this?" while holding up an incredibly decorative amulet.

The woman started telling stories about her ancestors while her eyes twinkled with knowledge. There are legends of a hidden city where the earth and stars meet, and people may communicate with spirits through old rites.

As they exchanged stories and looked for clues as to the whereabouts of the Star City, James and Carter found themselves in deep conversation with a group of local hunters.

By late afternoon, their bags were stuffed with memos, newly acquired items, and a lot of food. More crucially, their thoughts were racing with fresh leads and neighborhood information to guide their next move.

James suggested the group check into the Traveler's Oasis, a two-story structure of a charming colonial era, with white-washed walls and blue wooden shutters. It's located just a stone's throw from the bustling harbor, and the gentle sound of waves is ever-present. The inn boasts a terracotta roof, with rooms overlooking the busy streets below. Inside, the wooden ceiling fans circulate the salty sea breeze, and antique furniture reminds visitors of a bygone era. Local artwork and tapestries adorn the walls, adding a touch of African flair. The enormous Lake Tanganyika, with its waters sparkling in the setting light, was visible from this location on the outskirts of Kigoma town.

Carter and James set up their lodgings and unpacked all the equipment they had. At the same time, Alice located a quiet space in the inn's courtyard and organized the items they bought that day. She thought about the old woman's stories as her fingers traced the intricate patterns on the amulet.

A young man with an attentive gaze soon approached her while holding a notebook. He asked, gesturing to the relics, "You're studying the legends of the Star City, aren't you?"

With a hint of astonishment, Alice raised her head. "I am, and you are, too."

He introduced himself as "Kofi" and chortled warmly. "A historian specializing in this area's stories and ancient cultures. Interesting."

Alice found it very intriguing: "We're on the hunt for something significant, anything connected to the Hades Manifesto, and you could assist, Kofi."

Although Kofi's eyes only slightly enlarged, his curiosity was apparent. As their chat progressed, it became evident that this chance meeting might be crucial to their mission.

Alice and Kofi were conversing earnestly as the sounds of clinking drinks, laughter, and chitchat filled the dimly illuminated inn. The historian started to unfold a map of the area and pointed out numerous historical sites and locations of earlier rituals. Each has its tale, many interwoven with the history surrounding the Star City.

"I've gathered data about the Star City for years. It's a myth my grandfather told me," Kofi said, running his fingers over a spot south of where they were standing. "This area was once a ceremonial site that has largely escaped the attention of modern exploration. It could be connected to the Hades Manifesto."

"Mind if I join in? " Carter asked as he returned from the inn's kitchen with a tray of local treats.

Kofi shared a stack of old sketches and handwritten notes with the two, each page containing hints, insights, and puzzles waiting to be solved.

Their shared purpose and excitement for the hunt were palpable, indicating their alliance with Kofi was the missing link they needed. As night fell, their conversations became more focused. The puzzle pieces formed a clearer picture, guiding their next steps deeper into Africa's heartland.

The trio, having spent the entire night absorbed in their quest, found themselves surrounded by a maze of maps, sketches, and notes strewn across the table as the first rays of morning peeked through the gaps in the wooden shutters of the inn, creating a cozy environment.

Freshly baked bread and spice aromas filled the air as the neighborhood market started to come to life outside. Children raced around laughing as sellers set up their stalls, adding to the ambiance of a hamlet waking up.

"We should leave today, ideally by noon, if we want to reach the ritual ground by tomorrow night," said Alice, rubbing her sleepy eyes as she peered out the window.

A local guide named Jengo can take us there, Kofi said with a nod. He is knowledgeable about the challenging terrain and regional traditions. I will introduce you to Jengo myself.

Their expedition was taking shape, and the ceremonial ground that may house the next piece of the Hades Manifesto puzzle beckoned. The urgency of their quest weighed on them: time was of the essence. Kofi stepped out to find Jengo while Alice and Carter packed up their study materials.

The heat in the village increased as the sun rose higher in the sky. An old jeep, battered from years of negotiating rough African terrains, pulled up to the inn. Beside it stood Jengo, a tall man with skin bronzed by the sun and eyes that told tales of many adventures. "Kofi tells me you're looking for the ceremonial grounds," he said with a smile that revealed a set of pearly white teeth.

"Indeed, Jengo." Carter replied, "We're trying to unearth further proof regarding the Hades Manifesto."

Dr. Mathews, their steadfast mentor from the university, and Prof. Serrano, the renowned linguist who worked with Carter on several projects in the past, both flew to Africa upon hearing about the discovery, realizing the magnitude of what this could mean for the world and history, appeared on the horizon as they discussed the journey ahead.

"This discovery is too monumental to overlook," Dr. Mathews warmly welcomed Alice, adding, "We've come to contribute our knowledge and help whenever we can."

"The inscriptions you've discovered may be written in a dialect I've been looking at," Prof. Serrano continued. "This might be the game-changing discovery we've been looking for."

The trek to the ceremonial grounds, with the promise of finding ancient secrets, had become an assembly of great minds, all driven by the fascination of discovery. Their group had now increased, bringing together a team of experts poised to unveil history.

The group huddled around a large, weathered map on an old wooden table outside the inn as the late afternoon sun threw long shadows over them. Jengo pointed to a region marked with ancient symbols, his fingers tracing a path that wound through dense forests and crossed a river before reaching the ceremonial grounds.

Jengo suggested, his eyes fixated on the perilous path ahead, "We should set off before daybreak. The forest is dense, and we'd want to reach the river crossing before nightfall."

In command, Dr. Mathews declared, "We'll need supplies for at least a week. Food, water, tents, and any tools that could be useful for our investigation. Fortunately, the local market was recognized for its variety, selling everything from fresh vegetables to specialist instruments. Alice and Carter expected this and had already started compiling a list.

Kofi proposed, "I can ensure we obtain everything we need at a fair price, as I have contacts at the market."

Every little clue could be the key to revealing the secrets of the Hades Manifesto, so Professor Serrano and Alice sat down with the fragment they found as the group worked on preparations, eager to decipher more before the expedition started.

Kofi led the way, his familiarity evident as vendors greeted him warmly, some even with familial endearment. The bustling market of Lome was a sensory overload. The sounds of haggling blended with the alluring aroma of grilled meats and ripe fruits. A sea of vibrant fabrics fluttered in the wind, catching the eye at every turn.

While Jengo and Professor Serrano were preoccupied with acquiring specialized tools and local artifacts, their academic minds seeing beyond their mere utility, Carter and Dr. Mathews concentrated on the more practical purchases, stocking up on preserved foods, water filtration systems, and durable camping gear.

While admiring the beautiful beadwork on a necklace, listening intently to a musician play the kora, and even indulging in a local specialty of grilled plantains sprinkled with chili powder, Alice, sensing an opportunity, took a minute to immerse herself in the local culture.

We've got everything we need, plus a little extra," Kofi said as the team reassembled, burdened with bags and gear. "We've done our best to be ready."

As the sun started to drop, the sky was painted gold and red, a visual reminder of the adventure that awaited them deep within Africa.

After their successful day at the market, the team checked into Ama's Village Haven, in a village in Ghana; it was a more rustic but cozy inn located at the heart of the village. It was built using local materials, clay, and straw, offering an authentic experience. Each room is a separate thatched hut equipped with mosquito nets and simple wooden furnishings. At its center is a communal fire pit where guests gather in the evenings to share stories, often accompanied by village elders playing traditional instruments. Despite its modesty, the inn is known for the warmth of its hospitality and the delicious local cuisine prepared by Ama herself. Kofi had chosen it for its discretion and security. The inn's wooden walls were decorated with hand-painted murals that portrayed stories of ancient Togolese legends.

The team met in the inn courtyard under the soft light of lanterns to finalize their preparations. The route to the mythical Star City would take a lot of work. Maps were laid across the wooden table, fingers tracing paths and marking significant landmarks.

Kofi pointed to a location on the map and said, "My grandmother used to tell stories of an ancient city hidden among those hills. We should head to the northern section of Togo, near the border with Burkina Faso."

"Kofi's intel matches with some of the Manifesto's hints," Carter said, leaning in. "The city is there if it exists."

A lot is riding on this, Alice muttered to Dr. Mathews as she quickly glanced around the team and focused on his thoughtful expression.

"More than any of us can imagine," he said with a nod, "However, we owe it to history to learn this secret because we have a strong lead."

They all decided to get some rest early because tomorrow would be the start of their journey into the Togolese interior.

An innkeeper's gesture to wish them well on their journey included a little lad holding a basket full of fresh fruit and bread as Alice answered the soft tap as the first light of dawn peaked through the inn's shutters.

The lad timidly addressed her as "Madam Alice," giving her the basket and wishing her luck on her journey.

The inn came to life with morning sounds, and everyone knew the importance of the day ahead. She grinned, thanking him, and watched as he rushed down the corridor to carry more baskets to her colleagues.

Ropes, flashlights, first aid kits, and food items were carefully examined as the crew gathered in the courtyard. Carter coordinated with a local guide, Jean-Luc, who had been engaged to assist them in navigating the challenging terrain of northern Togo.

With Kofi and Jean-Luc in charge, the convoy started its slow migration out of the town, traveling toward the ancient hills with promises of undiscovered secrets, as Alice and Carter shared a short glance. This was the conclusion of years of research and hunting down tales.

Dust clouds trailed behind them as the sun rose in the African sky, and Alice tried her best to keep her journal steady on her lap, penning down ideas and observations. Occasionally, Kofi would point out a landmark or offer a piece of local mythology.

Carter, who had been quiet for most of the voyage, suddenly perked up when he saw the Koutammakou countryside spread out to the west, with its distinctive traditional mud tower houses known as "Takienta."

He enthusiastically said, "Do you know, Alice, those mud houses have been around for generations? The layout is practical, allowing for airflow while providing sun protection.

Alice grinned, always amused by Carter's propensity to transform any circumstance into an opportunity for a history lesson.

The team enjoyed the break, stretching their legs and enjoying the local fruits Kofi had brought along when they came to a dense grove of baobab trees, where Jean-Luc indicated the stop for a quick breather was needed. They set up a picnic under the cover of the trees.

Even though the situation was difficult at this early stage of the journey, the group's attitude was unwavering.

The party spread out on the woven mats under the shade of the baobabs, enjoying the sweet taste of the fruits and the break from the travel. At the same time, Kofi, the storyteller, started weaving a tale as the soft breeze rustled through the enormous tree leaves.

He started by saying, "Long ago, the Hades Manifesto was thought to be guarded by the 'Watchers of the Baobabs,'" his voice smooth and alluring. He pointed to their enormous trunks and said, "These trees were not merely landmarks but silent sentinels. It was thought that they were home to the observers' spirits."

"What were these watchers protecting against," further wondered Alice, her curiosity peaked.

Kofi said they were protesting unworthy searchers, leaning in to ensure he had everyone's full attention, like those who preferred domination and power to knowledge.

Despite his dubious expression, Alice's eyes were wide as she listened intently to everything Kofi said.

Every new narrative added layers to the mythology, increasing the mystique of their quest and transforming it from a simple item hunt into a pursuit of history, myths, and the spirit of Africa itself.

The afternoon sunbathed everything with a golden tint, producing long shadows that danced with the wind as Kofi continued his stories under the shade of the baobabs.

Kofi claimed that the Manifesto wasn't just a collection of writings or inscriptions. It was believed to be a living creature that changed and adjusted based on the intentions of its bearer.

Instinctively reaching for her small notebook, Alice listened closely, eager to jot down the specifics.

Kofi spoke reverently, "In the wrong hands, the Manifesto could lead to destruction beyond imagination, but in the hands of a person with a pure heart, it would guide its reader to a utopia, a paradise on Earth."

They had all heard of the tyrants and conquerors of history, and the prospect of one wielding the authority of the Hades Manifesto was horrifying.

"Why could something with such a strong potential for good have a negative side?" Carter questioned, clearly perplexed.

"That is the nature of true power, isn't it?" Kofi regarded him thoughtfully. "It shows the soul of the one who sees it. It's no difference with the Manifesto."

The weight of their mission was becoming increasingly apparent to Alice and the others, who experienced a mixture of amazement and dread as they realized both the promise of paradise and the possibility of destruction were now part of their path.

They were all gathered, thinking over the ramifications of Kofi's tales, each immersed in their thoughts, weighed down by the heaviness of the Manifesto's power. The twilight had fallen, and the horizon was aflame with brilliant reds and purples.

Alice dissolved the tension of this Manifesto possessing the capacity for both utopia and destruction by saying, "We have an even more outstanding obligation to find it. We must allow it to end up in the right hands."

"Kofi, where do we even start our search?" Alice asked. "Do we know anything about its last-known location?"

After a brief pause, Kofi went into the folds of his robe and pulled out a worn-out map, stating, "This is a map from my great grandfather's time," and set it down on the wooden table in front of them. It is rumored to serve as a marker for the locations of historical shrines that guard the way to the Hades Manifesto.

"This could be our next lead," Carter mumbled as he followed the lines, his gaze narrowing at a particular location deep in the Congo.

Kofi said, "But it won't be simple. Many people out there want to keep us from reaching the Congo, which is a vast maze."

With determination, Alice said, "Then we need to be ready. We start the next phase of our journey tomorrow."

The crew would advance further into the heartland, inspired by a feeling of purpose and the pull of the unknown, as the chance to find a world-changing item and defend it from people with evil intents was too great to pass up.

The Hunt for the Hades Manifesto had officially started as the crew prepared for the obstacles that lay ahead beneath the cover of the starry African night, unified in their mission and the bonds they were forming.

Chapter Three: Echoes of the Guardians

It was an ordinary day when Alice, Kofi, and Carter found themselves at the historic Silver Grove Forest border as dawn's first rays of light touched the Star City. The echoes of the past were all around them. The trees seemed like all the others from a distance; there was nothing out of the ordinary about them. Still, up close, their silver-hued bark was liquid and shimmered with a magical radiance in the early sun. This was no ordinary forest; if the legends were to be believed, it included the guardians as well.

Kofi saw a stranger standing on the same historic Forest's outskirts. Apart from the commotion at the border, her stare was clear, unwavering, and intensely intelligent. She seemed resolute in her persona. A flurry of mysterious symbols and suggestions surrounded her. She had thick black hair that framed her face, and she wore a silver pendant that glowed in dim light.

She greeted the team with a sweet yet authoritative voice, "Luna." When she noticed their puzzled looks, she chuckled and cleared her throat, "From the University of Delphi, I'm a linguist and historian. My area of study has been the linguistic analysis of historic sects." She smiled at the others.

She stepped closer to the group, exposing the pendant's pattern: two interwoven serpents around a rare antique glyph. Luna was the first one to speak, "I've been following the Hades Manifesto for years. "This pendant I wear has been handed down through my family for many years. According to legend, it once belonged to a guardian."

The group reacted with interest and distrust to her announcement. Luna was an asset because of her educational background; being an expert in extinct languages and her natural ability to crack codes might be the key to their success. She appeared out of nowhere; it was all too convenient as she hesitated at the grove's entrance. Luna muttered, "The Sentinels, ancient guardians of the grove and keepers of its secrets, are here."

Carter laughed, always the skeptic, "We're here for the Hades Manifesto, not bedtime stories, so stop telling us legends and fairy tales."

However, Kofi appeared far away; his gaze fixed on a strange tree marking that resembled the jewelry Luna was wearing. He said in a low, respectful tone, "My grandma told me about this very place. She noted the Sentinels were real and held the Manifesto's secret."

Always practical, Alice cut them off as they were talking and said, "If the Sentinels are actual, we must proceed with extreme caution because we are encroaching on their territory."

The quartet walked on, each step carrying the weight of the grove's past. The Silver Grove was only the first step into the archives of mystery; the mission to discover the secrets of the Hades Manifesto had truly begun.

As they traveled farther into their journey, the forest became denser. Every sound—including the distant bird calls and leaf rustlings— seemed intensified and carried the whispers of long ago. The air in Silver Grove was crisp and scented with rain and an archaic parchment aroma. Soft glowing scopes would periodically pass by, lighting up areas of their course before disappearing.

The Sentinels were offered a grasp of the secrets of the cosmos in exchange for their agreement to serve as its perpetual guardians.

Kofi was still far off somewhere else and, in a trance, as he frequently reached out to touch the silver bark in an apparent effort to make contact. Always on guard, Carter kept his hand close to the concealed handgun under his jacket. At the same time, the unnerving sensation of being observed tormented him.

They halted when Alice abruptly came to a stop. A complex stone archway with the same emblem Kofi identified on the keystone stood before them. In answer, Luna's pendant appeared to hum.

"This might be our first concrete hint," Alice murmured, her voice trembling with awe.

Shadows and reality merged in the forest beyond the arch as if welcoming them into the center of the Silver Grove's mysteries. As they proceeded forward, attracted by an overwhelming pull toward the Grove's center, the distinction between legend and reality faded.

There was uncertainty looming as the team paused at the archway's brink. The weight of many tales and warnings burdened them. As Luna took the first step, the light from her pendant became brighter, revealing the first few feet of a path that appeared to have emerged from the darkness.

"The Sentinels built these roads to protect the Silver Grove's heart, according to legend," Luna whispered. "We could get trapped in an unending maze if we take one wrong step. We must be careful."

Alice inhaled deeply and gave Kofi a cheery glance, "We trust in the route set out by the guardians and the knowledge of your ancestors."

Kofi's connection to Silver Grove grew stronger as they continued their journey. He heard hazy whispers that seemed to come from the past. The voices became increasingly audible as they descended, directing him as he decided his course of action.

Carter's uneasiness deepened in the meantime. He felt odd. Despite the forest's calm beauty, he couldn't shake the feeling that they were being watched. There was someone there with them. Are there occult watchers, ancient guardians, or something more sinister? Some spirits?

Unbeknownst to them, the first of the Sentinels' ancient eyes were watching from the canopy above. The old guardians of the forest knew that their trip into the heart of the Silver Grove had only just begun.

The vegetation lit up spectrally as they traveled deeper into the forest. Even though there was no breeze, trees were whispering tales of old as their leaves rustled. The charm of the Silver Grove was enigmatic and ancient.

Kofi started to murmur, his words blending with the echoing whispers. The mark on his wrist, formerly thought to be a birthmark, throbbed, and let off a weak light in time with the Grove's beat. He had a deeper bond with the forest than he ever recognized.

Luna approached Kofi after noticing the change in him and said, "The spirits of your ancestors are communicating with you. Pay close attention because they just might lead us to the Hades Manifesto."

Sentinel-like eerie forms were briefly visible to Alice as her eyes darted around, catching them moving between the trees. They were

32

being observed, but they weren't in danger. These Grove guardians were measuring their intentions to uphold the Grove's purity.

Carter stopped abruptly after hearing faint music. "Do you hear that?" he asked quietly. The song's captivating beauty drew them further into the center of the old woodland.

Following the music, they came to a clearing where a clear lake lay, its surface reflecting the stunning canopy above like a mirror. The lake's middle, where a stone platform rose and was ringed by lilies that twinkled like stars, was where the singing came from. It was suddenly louder.

A lady stood on the platform, her flowing robes the moon's color and her hair falling below her shoulders. Her voice seemed to blend with the very soul of the Silver Grove as she sang a beautiful melody.

"Who is she?" Alice said.

"The Siren of the Silver Grove, custodian of its deepest secrets and the melodies of the past," Luna replied in a hypnotic state. She loved the music.

The Siren stopped her song and gestured for them to proceed. Her voice resounded over the lake as she uttered, "Seekers of the Hades Manifesto, why are you in my territory? What brings you here?"

Kofi moved forward and raised his marked wrist as he sensed an unexplainable connection. "The Hades Manifesto and my bloodline are interwoven, and I seek answers."

She gave him a longing look as she regarded him, "Then, to proceed, you must demonstrate your worthiness. To reach the Manifesto, one of you must recite the Guardians' Song."

The task given was a tough one. The group looked at each other nervously. They had only just started their trip when they encountered an old test that may always tie them to the forest.

Kofi climbed onto the stone platform as the cool water lapped at his boots, feeling the weight of his ancestry on his shoulders. While Luna held onto the enigmatic jewelry she usually wore, the others anxiously awaited from the shore.

The Siren never took her eyes off Kofi. "Are you ready?" She asked in a melancholy whisper, "To mimic the song of the Guardians is to understand their anguish, delight, and sacrifices."

Kofi nodded resolutely.

Once more, the Siren began to sing, the sounds rising and falling like the waves of a midnight sea. Kofi closed his eyes as he felt the music surround him, trying to penetrate his very being.

Hours seemed like minutes. Kofi then started singing after taking a big breath. His voice, which was initially harsh, suddenly merged with the Sirens', harmonizing flawlessly, and evoking the sadness and beauty of long ago.

Luna, Carter, and Alice watched in bewilderment. As their voices blended, the woodland shimmered, vibrating in time. The Siren grinned as the last note vanished. "You may continue; the Guardians' echoes have found resonance in you."

A hidden way extending further into the Silver Grove was made visible when the waters separated. The next stage of their quest lay ahead, guarded by the ageless songs of the past and cloaked in ages-old mysteries.

When the passage was clear, Kofi led the team further into the Silver Grove's interior. The thick canopy discharged an eerie light that illuminated the pathway. Strange, glowing plants surrounded them, each seeming stranger and prettier than the previous. But what drew their attention was the deafening silence but the muffled sound of their footsteps.

They reached the old remains, the last stand of a long-gone civilization. Stories about the guardians, their duty as forest guardians, and their relationship with the Sirens were depicted in stone carvings. With her extensive knowledge of ancient symbols and languages, Luna noticed a recurrent character: a bird that resembled a phoenix, its wings protectively encircling a scroll that was the Hades Manifesto.

Luna rubbed her fingers over the weathered carvings and thought aloud, "The Guardians didn't simply guard the forest. They protected the knowledge, secrets many people wanted to know, but few did."

Drawing the engravings in a little notepad, Alice took it out. "It's not just about the physical trek but about the heritage of the Guardians, and we need to understand this relationship to locate the Manifesto."

They discovered a massive stone monument in a clearing and continued their journey with a big phoenix emblem in the middle. Our team became aware of their mission's importance when they realized they were getting closer to their goal. They were now guardians of an ancient legacy rather than only regular treasure hunters.

The ancient mystery of the stone monument stood solemnly in place. Kofi made a cautious approach since he felt an underlying intensity. Its surface was decorated with several circular depressions that looked like ornate locks.

Carter muttered, "We're at the threshold," as he saw Kofi engage with the memorial.

"The Sirens! They're not simply tied to the Guardians; they're the key," Luna shouted as she scanned the engravings. She pointed to one that depicted a siren singing, her notes lining up with the circular depressions.

"Do you mean the melodies we've heard that connect with the Grove?" Alice recalled their previous experiences and questioned.

"The next phase will be unlocked by singing the siren's song," Luna replied with a nod.

But this wasn't just any melody. It echoed time, a magical piece laced with Guardian memories. Kofi started humming as he closed his eyes, sensing the notes rather than remembering them. Slowly, a melody began to take shape, and as he struck the final note, the depressions in the monument lit up and began to pulse.

The ground shook slightly, and then a hallway appeared before them, inviting them to explore the Silver Grove's mysteries and reach the Hades Manifesto. The group looked at each other nervously; they hadn't anticipated how serious the hunt was getting, and this was all new for them.

The newly discovered passage wasn't gloomy. Instead, the ceiling was covered in bioluminescent vines that produced an ethereal glow. Every step they took echoed with an archaic significance.

Leading the way, Kofi felt compelled to go further down the passageway.

They occasionally came upon symbols carved into the stone, each signifying a particular protector. Being the scholar he was, Carter quickly noted each character in his notepad. His eyes lit up with wonder, "These might be the clues or a guide to navigating the Silver Grove," he mumbled to no one in particular.

Alice's acute hearing picked up a murmur in the distance, and she replied, "Do you hear that?" As she absorbed the vibrations by softly stroking the walls with her fingers, Luna nodded in agreement.

The passageway grew wider as they walked ahead, opening into a massive area with a center pool of clear water as its focal point. There were ethereal apparitions that danced beautifully from the pool's surface, depicting historical rituals and rites.

Luna exhaled and said, "Guardians," her voice was filled with awe as she continued, "This is their legacy—memories waiting to show their ancestry at the appropriate time."

As Kofi walked toward the pool, the water reflected his image and brief glimmers of the guardians conversing with his ancestors. The trip to the Hades Manifesto involved moving forward and plunging into the past. The solutions were entangled in the past and the present and were waiting to be uncovered.

Kofi, enthralled, hesitantly extended a hand to the water's surface. Memories sprang to mind as his fingers scanned the fluid. He noticed a guardian standing tall by a man who looked like him. With their united effort, they attempted to push the menacing force into the depths and seal it off.

He drew back, gasping, his head racing. "That was... one of my ancestors. He and a guardian sealed away a malicious force, something strong enough to endanger this entire realm."

Luna kept a close check on him as her eyes reflected the shimmer of the water. "By connecting with this pool, you've tapped into your ancestral memories. This pool might represent a nexus of recollections, a location where the past meets the present."

After that, Alice walked toward the pool, the waves twisting her reflection. The air was filled with urgent whispers that were too weak to be heard clearly. The energy of numerous memories was evident throughout the entire area.

From his notes, Carter examined them and raised his eyes, "The guardians and your ancestors collaborated to safeguard something essential we need to comprehend. These echoes take us deeper into the secrets of the Hades Manifesto."

They moved toward a small exit at the other end of the passageway as a soft breeze gently swept through it. Although the way appeared clear, the weight of history pressed down on them, making them again aware of their mission's seriousness.

The group emerged from the chamber onto a lush area lit by bioluminescent plants. The way ahead was littered with similar puddles of recollections, each one containing a different secret or tidbit of information.

"Every pool could contain another clue," Carter paused and said, "But we don't have time to study them all."

Luna stroked a small flower that gave out a gentle glow, "Every action we take in this place reverberates in the pages of The Hades Manifesto, which is more than just a book."

As they walked, a soft song resonated about them, becoming louder and more pronounced with each stride. It was a somber song with a thread of hope, like an old lullaby.

Kofi muttered, "The song of the guards," recalling the tune from his youth. It was sung to me by my mum."

Alice took a moment to feel the soft vibrations in the ground, "This location is a living archive that brings its stories to life with every sound and touch."

An imposing stone door with markings like those on Kofi's wrist stood near the end of the corridor. As she got closer, Luna touched it. In response to her touch, the symbols began to light brightly.

She guessed, "It's a doorway." The door slowly started to open, revealing the next stage of their journey. "But to where? Or when?" They were delving further into the center of old secrets as they searched for the Hades Manifesto.

A vast cavern could be seen as the stone door retreated. A massive tree with deep-rooted branches spread skyward and held glowing spheres in its units stood in the scene's center. The Silver Grove's power and link to the guardians came from this Tree of Echoes.

Kofi drew closer and saw writing on the tree trunk, each line lively with tangible energy. He muttered, "The history of the guardians," remembering some of the stories his mother told him.

Luna walked up to one of the glowing spheres and lightly touched its surface. Visions of guardians defending the city's inhabitants, standing firm against evil powers, and weaving sacrifice and victory into an eternal dance flooded her imagination.

With his voice faintly echoing in the void, Carter thought to himself, "We're not just retrieving a book. We're putting a legacy together."

A swooshing sound drew Alice's focus to the tunnel's edge. The Sentinels came out of the shadows, led by a guy with a dominating presence. "You've gone a long way," the leader said, "But more than reading about the past is needed to understand it."

He indicated the tree, "You can only fully understand the significance of the Hades Manifesto and its purpose via experience."

Kofi approached the Sentinel leader while maintaining his composure, "How would you have us experience it?"

One of the Sentinels responded to the leader's signal by moving forward while carrying a silver chalice that contained a shining elixir. "You can wander through the guardians' memories and comprehend the core of the Hades Manifesto by drinking this, which is the Echoes' Brew made from the sap of this tree."

Carter cocked an untrusting eyebrow. "How can we be sure that this isn't a ruse?"

"We came looking for answers, and this might be our only opportunity," Luna said, feeling a deep connection to the elixir.

Each group member took a sip from the cup gingerly, one at a time, starting with Luna. The environment changed around them as they were taken to a different era. They watched the guardians at their best, learned of the Hades Manifesto's beginnings, and experienced the weight of the sacrifices to secure its defense.

When they arrived back outside the Silver Grove, not in the tunnel, the sunrise had painted the horizon in golden hues. Only the memory of their interaction and a clearer understanding of their duty remained after the Sentinels had vanished.

They felt a sense of urgency because the guardians' echoes were carved in their souls. The Hades Manifesto was more than simply an artifact; it represented strength and optimism. A force that, in the wrong hands, might bring Star City's destruction.

After contemplating the thoughtful visions, Kofi finally spoke, his voice resonating with the weight of revelation. "This quest is more significant than us. The guardians trusted us to protect Star City from forthcoming disaster. We've been chosen not by chance but by destiny."

Alice reached down, the magic still lingering in her fingers, and said, "We have received knowledge from Silver Grove, but it is insufficient because we urgently need to locate the Manifesto."

The tension-filled air was mixed with urgency and hope. Carter, ever the planner, started to develop a strategy. "We move eastward toward the Labyrinth of Shadows, which, according to legend, contains a map showing where the Manifesto is buried."

Luna nodded as she thought, "Yes, but the Labyrinth is more than just a maze; it will assess our bravery, intelligence, and togetherness."

They gathered in a circle and stacked their hands before walking away. They had a strong solidarity made stronger by their common goal and newly acquired knowledge.

Kofi mumbled, "May the guardians direct our journey." The shadows awaited their arrival. Still, the echoes of the past and the promise of a terrifying future spurred them on. The group stood at the entryway, focused and together.

As the group got ready for the expedition, night fell upon the Silver Grove. In delicate contrast to the irresistible intensity, they just felt, the ethereal brightness of the Silver Grove trees showered them in brilliance. A small crystal the guardians had given Luna's ancestors as inspiration was taken from her pouch. "This will lead us through the deceit of the Labyrinth," she said.

Carter looked at an antique parchment with worn edges and almost faded symbols. Each obstacle in the Labyrinth represents one of the five elements: earth, air, fire, water, and spirit; we must overcome them to reach the inner sanctum.

Luna shivered as she investigated the Labyrinth's dark woodland. It was deeper than she had thought. The Labyrinth is more than just walls and puzzles; it is alive and conscious and can sense anyone approaching.

Kofi moved toward a big, old stone marked with the Guardians' emblem at the forest's edge as the last preparations were being made.

He touched it and felt the warmth of ages of caution. He said, "We are the echo of their legacy."

The shadows of the Labyrinth got closer with each step they took as they set out toward their destination, drawing strength and knowledge from the Silver Grove. Before them, the stone walls rose demoralizingly, whispering tales of those who dared to enter.

Chapter Four: Labyrinth of Shadows

It was a sunny day. The team had already tolerated oppressive desert heat, so the chilly gust of wind that met them at the cavern entrance was a sharp contrast to what they experienced earlier. The entrance was well-lit by moonlight, which reflected off the walls and caused them to sparkle like a starry night sky since they were covered in minerals. When Carter turned on his flashlight, the beam pierced the darkness and revealed the cavern's depth. He then adjusted his rucksack. As they descended, the sound of their footfall seemed to reverberate with ancient secrets. Looking back at the crew, Carter said, "Stay close and be careful. Ancient civilizations frequently left traps in cave systems like these to protect their secrets." After a pause, he added, "Keep a close eye on anything that looks different."

Eli walked through the shadows to join Carter in the foreground. His silent demeanor has been constant ever since he came to join them. He said, "I've been studying these caverns for years. And what I know about them is that there are stories, a lot of stories, about entire missions going missing. So, we don't know what might happen to us." Rhea quickly scribbled in her notebook after taking out a pencil, "These symbols are like a representation of an ancient ceremony with all these people dancing around a fire," she frowned and muttered, brushing her fingertips over the faded pictures on the wall. It was a mesmerizing experience for her.

Alice, clutching her backpack, inhaled deeply as she sensed the seriousness of their task. She knew she would have to be stronger than ever, to face all that lay ahead. The magnitude of what was in store was intimidating, and she was scared to an extent. In addition to danger, the legends of the labyrinth and the Hades Manifesto hinted at significant insights. Despite the unknown, the team continued, drawn deeper into the Labyrinth of Shadows with no protection or safety against the world.

As they walked inside the cavern, the walls enclosed them like a scary monster holding a child. Stalactites and stalagmites appeared to be about to close like the jaws of some ancient beast. Each breath they took echoed the pressure they felt as the air became colder and much denser. Alice frowned, having previously worked with relics from similar locations, and pouted, "Look at the precision. This entire maze was cut," claiming that the tunnels weren't formed naturally. "Was there an external force?"

"This labyrinth served as a place of worship and a fortress protecting its most sacred items. Like a guardian, too. The ancients who designed this place had the knowledge of which we can only dream."

Carter nodded in agreement as he found a device buried in the floor as the group negotiated a series of turns. A plate that is circular and has elaborate writing all over it appeared. He knelt and looked at it. "We should exercise caution, as this appears to be a trap."

Rhea's eyes narrowed as her fingers danced across the symbols. She said with a smile, "It's a test for those who wish to proceed. It's a puzzle. Like a mystery or something."

Then, their torches lit a painting on the opposite wall, which was partially hidden by the shadows. In the image, there were guardians standing solemnly, guarding a decorative chest that was surrounded by fire. There was text written beneath the picture.

"Only those with the fire of truth can pass unhurt," Alice had to squint her eyes to read that. It was a foreign language, and she had no trouble translating that.

Carter and Eli exchanged curious glances as they realized the labyrinth was more than a building. It was a monument to an ancient people's brilliance and noble attempt to preserve a force of immeasurable power. They really did their best to protect what they valued. The secrets of this location were connected to those of the Hades Manifesto.

Alice said, "this must be the Fire of truth," as she fixed her gaze on the mural, "Could it be a symbolic fire, like the enthusiasm or commitment to a cause? I am confused about this."

Eli said, "Or it may be literal, you know. You can take it as a test. You can pass if you have the genuine fire of truth; if not, you will perish."

The atmosphere became heavier as they felt not just the air pressure but that of their task weighing on them. The very walls were glowing with an eager energy. They were reminded of the secrets and risks hiding behind the maze with every step and every whisper. It was not a place they could call home.

Rhea took the initiative as the team moved slowly forward, carefully scanning every area for concealed devices or symbols. She could see minute imperfections in the walls and floor with her sharp vision and exclaimed, "Guys, there are patterns here. I just know there are.

The ancients wouldn't simply set a trap without giving the worthy a chance to figure it out. Everybody, come here. "Look!"

They gathered and observed what she pointed out. She was right; there was a pattern. The team encountered several chambers as they went deeper into the cavern. There were treasures in each one, relics from a long-gone era. The people who lived there in ancient times had left tools, pottery, and old writings skillfully placed as though they had been abandoned in the middle of usage. A tragedy had befallen them.

Carter abruptly came to a halt as his eyes widened in recognition. One of the pots was embellished with an iconic symbol, which he recognized immediately. He said hushed, "This... is the same insignia from my family crest," as the pressure of his ancestry and past made him realize where he was. He sensed a thrill of emotions across him.

Alice took note of his response and placed a comforting hand on his shoulder. "Hey, I understand what you are feeling. This trip teaches us more about ourselves than we ever imagined, not just the Manifesto. So, it's important. You must stay strong and composed."

Eli slowly nodded and said, "The Hades Manifesto is not the only thing the labyrinth defends; those who seek it have their identities torn apart. There seems to be a like price or something one must pay."

There was a congested path that opened into a vast chamber with pillars and bridges over all those bottomless pits. There were small cracks in the ceiling's surface, allowing rays of light to pass through, illuminating dust particles that had been motionless for so many centuries. A large pedestal with an old stone tablet above it stood in the middle of the room.

With her extensive knowledge of ancient sites, Luna addressed it with respect. She bowed slightly as her voice echoed, "This...this is old, even by this labyrinth's standards. I am sure about it." She tried to decipher the hidden message.

Rhea sat by her side, her perceptive eyes noticing patterns Luna's knowledge may have missed. She pointed to something that looked like the North Star, a map for travelers.

Eli, who had previously shared his discoveries with Dr. Moreau, saw this as a brilliant opportunity to contribute. "Perhaps this is another sign or direction for our quest," he remarked, "as many ancient cultures felt that labyrinths were not merely physical trials but spiritual journeys. So, we can assume that this one is the same, right?"

A sudden soft clink followed a quiet rumble. Unknowingly, Jacqueline had stepped on a floor switch. It could be a dangerous thing, with all the unknown puzzles. The team looked at each other in a horrified expression as they realized that this could mean disaster. The crew was put on high alert right away. Before they could react, a portion of the floor began to pull back, exposing a staircase that descended and was dimly lit by an unknown light source.

Carter took the initiative without hesitation, motivated by his earlier realization of the connection to his family. He went down the stairs, the others soon after he started to descend. They knew the subsequent labyrinth level would evaluate their mental resilience and physical might.

The mood grew more oppressive with each step they took down the long, winding staircase. They marveled at the mosaics with elaborate designs adorning the walls depicting scenes of historical wars, celestial bodies, and all those strange characters. Each tile contained a unique story since their colors were still brilliant even after so long.

The mosaic of a woman with flowing hair carrying a scroll resembling the Hades Manifesto caused Alice to pause briefly and examine it. She wondered aloud, her mind making associations with the legend of Hades, "This might be Persephone."

Eager to impart his historical knowledge, Eli said with a hint of arrogance in his tone, "Could Persephone be the Guardian this labyrinth refers to? Persephone, in some legends, was not simply a passive character but a custodian of wisdom. So that means Persephone could be the guardian that this labyrinth is referring to."

Rhea saw a strange tile just slightly elevated above the others as she continued to look for hidden threats or clues. She whispered her remark to Luna, being careful not to wake the others, and motioned for Carter to join her. The three gathered while deliberating whether to press the issue.

Jacqueline took a little detour while they talked, mesmerized by a painting of constellations. One star cluster reminded her of something she had seen as a child. And when she began to understand it, it also triggered an unwanted recollection from her past connected to the danger they were about to meet.

Jacqueline's fingers shook as she traced the constellation, which felt all too familiar. Instead of three stars making Orion's Belt, four stars were in the star formation, slightly altering Orion's appearance. The last time she had seen this altered constellation was on an ornament she had been given as a young girl. Her grandmother had owned the pendant, which was a mystery in her family's past. Everybody knew they were tied to antiquity's hidden societies.

She said, her voice a mixture of fear and wonder, "It can't be..."

Alice approached Jacqueline after hearing her, her eyes flitting between the mural and her face as she realized what was going on. She said, "That constellation, it's unusual. I've found references to it in several obscure writings; they always make vague references to a subterranean room or a portal of some kind."

Eli swiftly interjected after overhearing their chat, saying, "This changed Orion could be the key, you know, like a blueprint or a path throughout this labyrinth."

Rhea let it sink in and suggested, "We should integrate these results. The raised tile might represent a switch, and this constellation might direct its users. It could have all the information from the raised tile."

As the group deliberated their next move, a chilly breeze carrying an evil air and a whisper came from farther into the labyrinth. The voice's apparent summons drew them into unknown depths, which cast a spell.

Deeper down the cave, the strange voice having ancient resonance could be heard. It sounded familiar to Carter, like a spectral echo from his stormy past. He had already experienced labyrinths, and this was not his first time into the occult. Carter had previously made his way through the dangers of Paris catacombs, where he first met Jacqueline and Rhea.

Rhea, who worked as a curator at the Louvre, was renowned for her photographic recall and superior expertise in antiquity. And when Carter first met Jacqueline, she was a young historian. They were bonded in a professional friendship that went on for more than ten years because of her passion for discovering the truth and their shared respect for Carter's knowledge and expertise. He really was an expert at what he did.

"Carter, hey, do you remember the catacombs? The inscriptions we found there. They hauntingly match the ones here, don't they?" Jacqueline recalled their first meeting and said with curiosity.

"You are right. The similarities are uncanny; I'd give it that." Carter remarked, "We must go carefully since the last time we encountered symbols like this, they led us to a room of danger and truths. This time, we need to be extra cautious."

Suddenly, a gentle glow with rhythmic pulses appeared farther inside the labyrinth. "That might be our compass," Eli said while maintaining his cool.

The voice became louder as they traveled further, leading, seducing, and revealing all those long-buried secrets.

The glow's origin was right in front of them, lighting up a vast circular room. It was covered in elaborate sculptures from several historical periods and civilizations that blended seamlessly while presenting a macabre dance between loyalty and betrayal.

Always attentive, Kofi held a notepad and sketched the symbols he observed. He was quick with his fingers. His knowledge of ancient languages was unmatched, and his proficiency in cryptanalysis made him extremely valuable. His forehead furrowed in concentration as he said, "This language... It's a mix of Greek, Latin, and something far older than all that."

Luna analyzed the room's layout with her ability to recognize spatial patterns. She was born with it. She observed the way that chamber was constructed and said, "It feels like it can rotate."

"I've read about such architectural designs. It's like a protection system, and we might need to align some portions to open our path," Alice interrupted.

Rhea moved toward a mural that featured a shadowy figure that resembled the mysterious figure they had previously encountered. "This is our key to understanding the Hades Manifesto," she said to everyone.

The team's previous confrontations with dark factions seeking power were all too vivid in their thoughts. Carter said, "But it's also a beacon for our foe. I mean, isn't that a risk or something?"

With a determined look, Jacqueline turned to face everyone. "We must immediately unravel this maze to understand and preserve the Manifesto. Isn't that our purpose?"

The team nodded and turned their attention to their task. The air in the chamber got chilly. Rhea and Jacqueline approached the fresco, their past as collaborators apparent in their coordinated motions. They had spent years studying the complexities of archaeology.

Rhea muttered, pointing to a person in the mural, "This...looks like...I think, oh no, I am sure this is Pythia." Pythia, the senior priestess of the Temple of Apollo at Delphi, was reputed to have prophetic powers. But why this place?

"The Hades Manifesto was about power in the physical sphere and mastery over time," Kofi remarked with a smile.

Luna noticed it resembled the Orion constellation when tracing a route on the ground. Her eyes twinkled with delight, "Guys, this looks like an alignment here. This chamber must revolve when the stars are positioned properly."

"But we do not really have the luxury of waiting for all those heavenly motions and whatnot. There needs to be a manual override," Alice continued.

Carter discovered the device, which was concealed by several stones. He said in a muffled voice, "This demands a specific order. We can't be careless about it."

Everyone realized Jacqueline was referring to the team's collective experience when she said, "Looks like our enemy is lined up to confront their most difficult problem yet."

The threat posed by their pursuers became more obvious as they worked on the challenging alignment. They drew nearer to the danger with each step they took into the labyrinth's center.

The tough technique of arranging the stones required complete focus. The room's chill and the heat of the perceived intensity were seriously different from each other. Rhea's quick fingers relocated one stone as she made calculations based on the cosmic patterns they had seen earlier in their trip.

Standing beside her, Jacqueline recorded each shift, capturing it in her photographic memory and linking it to earlier discoveries she had seen. "Remember Rhea, the Orion cipher we discovered at the Alexandrian library?"

Kofi, who was standing nearby, started humming a melody before Rhea could answer. It wasn't arbitrary. The tune was old and believed to have origins in Greek mythology. He sang, "Listen to the rhythm of the stars."

To compare the celestial design with her understanding of star systems, Luna stared at the mural for a long time. She connected their current position to the larger mythos of the Manifesto, "The ancients thought that Orion was chasing the Pleiades. Interesting. Very interesting."

Alice considered escape routes because she was always a realist, "No matter what we find here, we must be ready to move quickly." She darted her eyes across the passages that could help them if necessary.

Carter maintained his meditative attitude throughout their mission. He wondered, his fingertips tracing the outer corners and carvings of the mural, "Every layer we peel back on this search makes me question how deep the roots of the Hades Manifesto truly run. It is fascinating yet dangerous."

As they investigated the mystery further, the situation became more intense; with each new finding, the labyrinth altered the celestial calculations and unlocked a sequence, which forced the entire group to readjust. There were old cobwebs and dust partially lifted to disclose a hidden chamber where the atmosphere was still and frozen in time. A bronze astrolabe, an essential part of understanding the Hades Manifesto, was displayed on a pedestal in the center of the room.

Alice walked up to it with caution and said, "I've read about these," sounding both in awe and alarm. They may be keys to other secret chambers but were employed for astronomical measurements.

After feeling the weight in her pocket, Jacqueline took out a small device. She kept it a secret ever since the events in Alexandria. This might be its pair, she finally admitted after a brief pause.

Rhea started lining up the tiny instrument with the bigger astrolabe since she was always the curious one. Combined, the complex engravings on both painted a picture of Hades and his control over the underworld.

Kofi's eyes grew wide. He declared, "This is more than just history. It's a tale of dominance, power, and betrayal."

As she looked around the space, Luna spotted a pattern on a far wall. "Is this what it is, Dr. Williams?"

"It's the Gate of Prophecy, Luna. Just so you know, we are closer to the Manifesto's heart than ever before," Carter said after taking a deep breath.

The crew then realized that the stakes had just become incredibly high due to that revelation. Being closer could mean being closer to risks. A concentric circle sequence was shown on the bas-relief engraving of the Gate of Prophecy. Each layer had elaborate patterns and symbols, some recognizable and others mysterious.

Suddenly, Rhea felt the cool metal seeping into her fingertips as her fingers lingered over the outermost ring. She said, "My grandmother used to teach me such figures. It's a story of forbidden love, entangled fates, and cosmic upheaval. These symbols are ancient Theban."

Alice frowned intently as her knowledge of historical linguistics became increasingly important. She gestured toward the middle of the gate, "Look here. The theme of Hades and his dominion of the underworld is present in the repeated line, 'From chaos, order is born.'"

Jacqueline examined all the matching symbols while closely looking at the smaller device she was carrying. The labyrinth shook as a faint trail that led further into the shadows lighted when it was aligned right next to the gate.

Luna whispered to Carter in a muffled voice, who had an eerie sense of space, "This place isn't just a relic; it's alive, nearly sentient. It has a soul of its own, you know. Can you feel it?"

Nodding, Carter said, "Oh yeah. I agree. Absolutely. The Hades Manifesto is more than simply a book or fiction; it is a synthesis of ancient power and knowledge that will fiercely preserve its secrets. It means that we must proceed with caution."

Kofi was wearing a family heirloom pendant around his neck in a tight grip. "We're currently in its lair; from what I can see, we're not the only ones. There are others, too."

The wavering glow from their candles added to their doubt, and the echoing sounds of the maze confirmed his suspicion. They moved forward with a common goal, but they were cautious since there were shadows everywhere in the maze. The illuminated path appeared to breathe, enlarging, and contracting like a human lung. Every step they took echoed with menace, highlighting their instability. Despite that, the appeal of solving the Hades Manifesto's secrets was strong for them.

Alice regularly paused to record the mysterious symbols in her journal because they fascinated her. She said under her breath, "These suggest rites of passage. It could be the process of becoming a manifesto guardian."

Kofi wondered aloud, "Or maybe it describes those judged worthy of knowing its power," after noticing a curious regularity to the patterns on the walls.

Jacqueline's keen eyes saw a minor detail, which was a jewel with a strange brilliance that was embedded in the ceiling. When she touched it, it revealed a fresco, illuminating the hallway in a cerulean radiance. Rhea and Jacqueline carefully examined it.

"The painting showed gods, humans, and other celestial beings dancing with creation and destruction. It's the dance of life and death, a balance kept by the guardians of the Manifesto," Rhea said as she ran her fingers down the figures.

Luna intervened and added, "This place wasn't just a maze or testing field."

Grimacing, Carter nodded in agreement. "We might never leave if we are judged unworthy at every turn we make and with every puzzle we solve."

A low growl that resounded in the distance warned them of the hazards ahead. The labyrinth's entry appeared miles away, yet its conclusion was tantalizingly close.

They had a long way to go on their journey through the night. But with each step, the significance of their mission became more apparent, and the weight of their responsibility increased.

The path's current downward slope signaled the beginning of the "Descent into the Abyss."

The group moved further into the center of the labyrinth. Subtly, the environment changed: the air became more relaxed, the shadows grew longer, and the silence deepened. With her innate ability to detect changes in the atmosphere, Rhea caught a throb of energy under their feet. She muttered reverently, "There's a heartbeat to this place. I can feel it, and it's so real."

Jacqueline said, "I feel it, too. It's as if the labyrinth itself is alive, watching and waiting," drawing on her intuition.

They entered a large room lined with a lot of large mirrors that reflected fragments of the past rather than the present. Alice was engrossed in a significant archaeological discovery as she remained motionless, her reflection showing a younger version of herself. Luna's mirror showed her holding a baby under a red moon, while Kofi's showed him participating in a traditional ceremony.

Carter hesitated for a while before facing his reflection with courage. A younger Carter reflected on a time when he had to choose between duty and love, which altered his life's course. It was not easy for him.

Luna said to Carter, "To embrace the challenges ahead, we must face our past."

The exit from the chamber was eventually seen, but it was more than just a doorway. A doorway of some sort, it was a spinning vortex that marked the conclusion of this chapter for our team and the start of a new chapter with new difficulties.

The weight of their task pushed heavy on their minds as they prepared to venture into the unknown; Carter guessed, "It's a doorway. The descent to the Abyss awaits."

Ever the defender, Kofi approached the portal gingerly before the party ventured through it, throwing little stones into its swirl to ensure safety. On the opposite side, they didn't reemerge after they vanished. The enigma widened. As the needle of an old compass approached the vortex, Jacqueline took it out of her backpack. Whatever went in didn't come out.

Dr. Alice Moreau said, "It's a trip across time,".

Rhea's eyes twinkled; she knew that her knowledge of mythologies from the past was timelier than ever. According to tradition, portals like these connect our world to the underworld, where truths are hidden in riddles, she said, her voice resonating with the weight of ancient tales.

Jacqueline gave her a sly look. She said in a muffled voice, "The Hades Manifesto."

"We need to be ready for what is ahead. Old tales imply difficulties and puzzles guarding the entrance to the underworld," Carter said, nodding his head.

After a deep breath, Luna moved toward the portal and tried to touch it. The spinning became more intense as soon as her fingers touched it, luring her in. There was too much of a draw.

They moved into the: "Descent into the Abyss" as a group, the world behind them disappearing as they did so.

The difficulties presented by the labyrinth had only just begun; what they didn't know was that the actual search for the Hades Manifesto was about to start.

Chapter Five: Whispers in the Wind

The breeze and the air whispered some dark and ancient legends as the last dusk colors covered the vast desert landscape. Each sand particle beneath their feet contained a lot of stories waiting to be found. The group had traveled far into tribal lands from the Labyrinth of Shadows. They realized that the weight of their mission was more significant with each step.

The team experienced something absurd as they traversed the vastness of the desert with its motionless sandbanks and all those distant horizons. They really felt they were close to discovery because of the Indigenous tribes' oral tales.

It was Elara who set up the camp close to an old rock formation. She played a melody from the area on her guitar to crack the musical code. She thought it contained information about where the Manifesto was. Carter was intensely focused on his notes when he randomly glanced at Elara. As they attempted to piece together the history, Luna, Rhea, and Jacqueline talked with some of the tribe's elders. Kofi kept guard in the shadows, constantly vigilant and on the lookout.

They would travel a route no one could have anticipated due to the ancient tales intermingled with the hunt for the Hades Manifesto. The price for sharing the desert's darkest secrets would be high.

The desert night came to life as Elara began to play her guitar. The clan elders started singing as the campfire's flickering light illuminated their faces. Old and knowledgeable, their voices told stories of gods, heroes, and lost treasures. Each line had a suggestion hidden beneath the sands, ready to be discovered by the chosen people. Fascinated, Alice danced her fingers over her tablet casually as she captured the rhythms and melodies. Knowing the significance of each syllable and every accent for archaeology, Dimitris leaned close beside her.

"The songs tell of a period when all the gods could roam among humans, and the mortals dared to confront the sky," said one elder, his voice like gravel. Their secret to success was 'The Hades Manifesto.'

"Does the location of the Manifesto appear in these songs," Jacqueline wondered, her attention piqued.

"The songs are not maps but guides," the elderly man hesitated and then spoke again, looking away, "You must merge with the desert to comprehend them. Pay attention to its stories and whispers."

Nearby, Carter and Kofi shared a knowing nod as they realized this journey was more than just discovering a relic; it was about gaining access to the past's knowledge to influence the present and future days. There was a lot at stake.

The desert's silence was occasionally broken by the soft rustling of the wind and the hypnotic rhythm of tribal drums. Still, Luna managed to catch the rhythmic pattern and realized it wasn't just random beats - it had a structured sequence. As night fell, the constellation-filled sky looked like it had a lot of tales to tell.

"I have been recording the songs' melodies and lyrics," Dimitris said, "The desert has its language. It is sung rather than written or spoken. The solution may lie in these indigenous tunes."

"Listen to this," Alice said as she slowed down a recording she made. Elara's eyes widened in recognition as she heard that the background beat hinted at a pattern or a code when slowed down. She looked amazed and fascinated at the same time.

"The elder warned me that the desert defends its secrets fiercely. Not all who search will find, and not all who find will return," Rhea said as she walked up to where the team was, her face cast in shadow. It served as a strong warning that risk lingered even amid the allure of discovery. Every step the team took was a dance with fate because the desert was as dangerous as it was beautiful.

The group gathered closer due to their shared enthusiasm for discovering the answers to the desert's secrets. Luna continued to beat her fingers in time with the tune. "Hey, I am sure it's Morse code," she recognized at once. "The style is Morse, but the rhythm is ancient and coded."

Everyone in the group shivered. It was overwhelming to consider the prospect of an ancient culture employing a style of communication resembling Morse code.

"It might not be Morse as we know it; cultures generate their own codes and patterns, and it is human nature to find order amid chaos," said Carter, ever the voice of reason.

Luna concentrated hard on deciphering. "After minutes that felt like hours, she eventually looked up. Whether Morse or anything else, this sequence repeats, indicating a westward direction towards the sinking sun."

The desert had a mind of its own - it reacted to their finding as a warning, as a gust of wind carried sand and whispers. Jacqueline, who was calmly observing, murmured, "We must respect the wishes of the desert. Also, remember that our perseverance and respect will define our fate. So, we need to be careful."

The expanse of the desert became more apparent as the team moved westward. The eternally extending dunes produced waves of golden grains under the merciless heat. They were constantly teasingly close to the horizon.

Elara led the way while carrying a compass. "We really need to be careful," she said. "Deserts can be misleading, and we may easily get lost. It's simple and easy. But with caution, we can avoid it. If we do get lost, we may starve to death, or who knows what might happen."

They had been moving for hours, and they were exhausted. Their homemade coverings and supplies that they had barely provided enough shade as the heat increased the temperature. Rhea, who was always observant, abruptly stopped and focused farther away. There is a caravan many hours away.

"Nomads? Here, in this harsh terrain?" Carter questioned with a squint.

"They are more accustomed to the area than any map or compass," Rhea said, nodding. "They are conversant in their language."

"We might draw some understanding from them, perhaps even guidance," Elara added.

With sweat on her forehead, Jacqueline groaned, "And hopefully, a bit of a break from this heat."

They all wanted a break. They would go up to the nomads with no idea about the rumors of their search that had already spread throughout the desert when they arrived at the caravan.

The hours passed, the sun started to set, and the silhouette of the caravan came into focus. Against the golden tone of the desert, a line of camels, flanked by tents and little fires, presented an enticing sight.

Kofi broke the silence and asked, "These nomads, don't they pass on stories or oral traditions? They know something, and if we ask them. Can we ask them? I have a strong feeling that they do know some old tales."

"Yes, generations of knowledge and memories have been stored—not on paper, but rather in the minds of the elders." Alice nodded with a smile. She liked the idea of talking to a nomad.

As they got closer to the camp, they were greeted by nomadic guards covering their faces with scarves, and only their eyes were visible. Although there was apparent hostility, Luna managed to greet them in their language, utilizing her mastery of language. She used an extra polite tone. The guards appeared surprised, and a murmur of admiration quickly passed around the group.

She was an older woman with wrinkles on her face but hawk-like eyes. "I'm Amina," she declared, "We are aware of your journey here. All of you."

"We come in peace and seek your wisdom," said Alice as she moved closer and held out her hand. It was a submissive act of surrender.

Amina glanced at Alice before indicating for the team to follow. The promises of revelation weighed heavy in the air, offering their objective a new level of intrigue: "Tonight, you will join us. The desert has many tales; perhaps the one you seek is right here within our songs."

The group made themselves at home and comfortable among the nomads under a blanket of sparkling stars. The shadows from flickering fires danced to the beat of the desert night. The team was starving after their travels, and even though a feast was being prepared, they could sense its importance.

Amina went to the central fire, where Elara was absorbed in the notes she had scribbled down after conversing with the elders. Amina pointed to an elderly man seated cross-legged beside the fire and holding a traditional stringed instrument.

She introduced Salim, the most renowned storyteller and musician in their tribe.

Elara gave a respectful nod while showing her interest. As Salim started to strum, a mesmerizingly lovely tune erupted. The notes had a narrative, echoing stories of loss, joy, and desert mysteries. The group was transfixed by the rhythm.

Elara's eyes widened in recognition as the final note reverberated. The melody followed a pattern and had a particular beat that felt comfortable. She whispered to Alice, "It's a code," her enthusiasm was very audible in her voice.

Amina gave a knowing smile. "Some stories we tell are just like keys, only waiting for the perfect door, Dr. Moreau."

Only the crackling of the fires could be heard as an abrupt silence descended upon the camp. Amina leaned forward, the flames casting a light on her face. She spoke in a soft voice, "Only a few of our tribe's members comprehended the song's significance, which is thought to convey the location of a long-lost oasis that may hold information relevant to your search."

Kofi's eyes glowed with enthusiasm as he said, "Do you think there could be a hidden copy of the Hades Manifesto somewhere out there?"

With a husky yet powerful voice, Salim intervened. "The oasis is said to be like a crossroad between realms and a sacred location that is guarded by the ancients, so it is more than just a location of water in the desert, guys."

Carter leaned closer and continued to listen closely. "If it's a fork in the road, it might be the key to opening the way to the Manifesto," he exclaimed with excitement.

Jacqueline questioned in a cynical voice, "With such tales, surely someone tried. Why hasn't anyone gone there before?"

Amina sighed, the weight of the tribe's past visible on her face as she said, "Many people have attempted to follow the song's trail. Still, some of them never succeed because of how extensive and complex the desert is."

The darkness grew darker than it was as everyone felt the pressure of the fresh revelation by Amina. Looking for the Manifesto was entwined with a lot of perilous regional myths.

Dimitris started connecting archaeological dots with Amina's tales by putting them together using his intelligence.

He rubbed his chin thoughtfully and added, "If I remember correctly, certain old Sumerian tablets referenced a desert intersection. The tales were correlated with astronomical alignments. But that's not all. The oasis is referred to as the Eye of the Desert."

Alice commented after thinking for a while, "If it's an accurate site, then we should be able to determine its location using the correct coordinates by comparing it to old star charts."

Elara hummed the tune of the tribal song while jotting down notes, remaining engrossed in her deciphering. She muttered, "The music seems to contain some phonetic codes, but I need more time to continue deciphering."

The team gathered closer as the night grew darker and a bit colder. Rhea came closer while holding a tattered leather map. She gestured to a collection of mysterious symbols and hazy lines on the map, saying, "This belonged to my great-grandfather. He was obsessed with the oasis."

"Is it a constellation?" Kofi questioned with squinting eyes.

"Orion," Carter nodded, "It is known to have been a significant constellation in ancient times."

"The belt of Orion always points to something major, right?" Luna suddenly interrupted with her question.

The group understood they had several parts of a giant puzzle. The tricky part was fitting them together coherently to light their way.

"Who would've thought the stars would be our GPS in this era? It feels like they are our personal satellites." Jacqueline chuckled, as she always found humor, even in stressful situations.

Amina made a trail on the map with her fingertips, with what she knew about the desert as a natural habitat. "Our forefathers always thought that following the Belt would lead you to the heart of the desert. Orion's Belt points towards the west from here at this time of year."

Elara measured the distance between their current location and the potential oasis with her fingers on the map. "The song mentions taking three steps to the west and dancing with shadows before the eye appears." She added after she was done with her math.

Kofi started deciphering the symbols around the map's margins using his knowledge of ancient languages. These inscriptions held the value of night, shadows, and the phase of the moon.

"What if it means we should travel in the direction Orion's Belt points, but only at a particular moon phase, using its shadow as a guide?" Alice suggested with a pout.

Carter added, intrigued by Alice's observation, "It might be a timed occurrence. The oasis, or its entry, is only visible or accessible under specific cosmic circumstances. It's not like a year-round thing that one can observe any time, any day."

Luna, who had quietly listened to the team's conversation, walked over to the map, and looked thoughtful. She pulled out her journal and turned to a page designated by a dried desert flower, muttering, "Moon phases." The carriers had complex drawings of the night sky with extensive commentary.

She pointed to her diagrams and said, "Look, over the past three nights, I've been tracing the moon's movements. Tomorrow night will be a waxing crescent, which casts a particular shadow, perfectly aligning with the tribal melodies," Elara translated quite easily.

"So, not only do we have a direction from Orion's Belt, but also, we have a definite time range during which the oasis might reveal itself," Dimitris remarked, "fascinated by the celestial connection."

Amina agreed by nodding and said, "The desert guards its secrets, disclosing them only to those who properly understand its rhythms, as the proverbial old tales have it."

"It's like a dance, a choreography of the cosmos," Kofi said, his face glimmering with knowledge. "Every step, every moment, everything has to be in perfect harmony for the secret to be revealed."

"Then tomorrow night is our moment. We prepare tonight and follow the dance of the desert under the crescent moon," Jacqueline said with a hopeful expression on her face.

The campground was bustling with activity as the group prepared for the mission that night. The heroes split the supplies among themselves and held torches while tightening camel saddles. Evening air in the desert carried a hint of expectation and a whisper of untold mysteries.

Elara practiced the tribal song leading their voyage while sitting cross-legged. There was an instant connection to the environment as the soft tune blended with the wind.

While conversing with Dimitris about the route, Carter checked the star charts and maps. They were on the right track thanks to the archaeologist's keen intuition and the scholar's extensive terrain knowledge and expertise.

Alice spent some time with Amina as the night became darker and the crescent moon started to rise. Throughout their brief acquaintance, their relationship had deepened, and the doctor's respect for the chief could be felt.

Alice acknowledged, her voice expressing sincere thanks, "We owe you a great deal."

Amina softly grinned. "Tonight, we walk in harmony with the echoes of the past. The desert is vast and unpredictable, but if we are together, we could just unravel its mysteries."

Standing next to each other, Rhea and Jacqueline looked around at everything and everyone. They understood the expedition ahead. It would be both testing and enlightening.

With only the torches they were carrying and the faint glimmer of the crescent moon above them, the caravan started to move. Elara's gentle strumming and camel hooves on the sand served as the group's guiding lullaby. It was an indication of their synchronicity with the environment.

Since the interpretation of the tribal song, Luna had been unusually quiet. Suddenly, she walked over to Elara. Luna asked, in a low whisper, "Do you feel it?"

 Elara paused her strumming and gave her a puzzled look. As she pressed her hand to the earth, Luna said, "The vibration, the resonance. It is as though the ground underneath us is responding to your music. Do you feel it now?"

Elara hesitated before picking up her oud again and focused by shutting her eyes. Soon, a gentle hum—a counter-melody—emerged from the depths of the desert as the notes appeared to move with the air.

With the critical eyes of a journalist, Jacqueline started taking pictures of the event. She said, "It's like the song isn't simply a map; it's a key."

Kofi took Carter's arm as he realized how serious the situation was. "The Manifesto might be more than just a book. We're not just looking for a place, are we? It's about understanding, resonance, and harmony. It's like developing some personality traits."

With each stride and each note, the Hades Manifesto's mystery grew more complex, blending history and present into a dance that was waiting to be solved.

Carter had to stop the caravan as it went through the vast area because the humming from below became increasingly intense. The hum and Elara's song blended to form a hauntingly lovely symphony that echoed through the night air. It was mesmerizing yet disturbing at the same time.

Dusting off an antique artifact, Dimitris commented. "What if the Hades Manifesto is more than just a document and serves as a testament to resonance and harmony? The songs, the stories... they've always emphasized unity. Isn't that a message or something?"

The realization that they weren't just looking for a relic but also a concept—a harmony that had been attained in the past but had since been lost—was overwhelming for all of them.

Usually skeptical, Rhea added with excitement in her voice, "It might be the most significant archaeological discovery in history and provide philosophical insight."

Alice expressed worry to Kofi as she was lost in thinking. As if on cue, a distant mirage shimmered, exposing dark people watching the group. "If it's that significant, there would be those who would try to misuse it." Was it a trick of the desert or a foreboding warning of betrayal? It was hard to figure out.

The seriousness of their mission became even more apparent; the hunt was about more than just finding things; it was about maintaining a sacred equilibrium.

The caravan's shadow spanned far into the horizon as the sun began to set. It painted a landscape of oranges and purples. Elara's recently discovered song from the tribes, which was melancholy and haunting, flowed freely and was borne by the wind. It echoed in the passages and told the tales of the legends.

Carter experienced an odd pulling sensation that drew him deeper into the enormous dunes. He walked over to Dimitris, who was feverishly drawing related patterns. Dimitris lowered his gaze and mumbled, "You feel it too, don't you, Carter?"

Carter nodded and said, "I do. It's like the desert is pulling us, sharing its memories."

Luna pieced together a story about a lost city that implied the location of the Hades Manifesto from a distance while immersed in tribal traditions and local culture.

Despite their disagreements, Jacqueline and Rhea were able to get along because they had an eerie sense of connectedness to their environment. They exchanged knowing looks as they realized the earth below carried more than just artifacts—it also had memories of an earlier time and a lot more than they knew.

The numerous campfires in the broad desert stood in stark contrast to the chilly, uninteresting, starry sky above. In the presence of tribal elders, Alice paid close attention, sifting through their words for cues or unspoken details regarding the Hades Manifesto. Her fingers brushed against the pendant, which was cold and strangely fashioned like an antique seal and given to her by a tribe woman.

Kofi could detect slight changes in the wind's direction, the sand flakes warning of looming danger. He noticed that the shimmering shapes in the shadows weren't just mirages but something more profound, darker. The nomadic chieftain Amina cautioned, her voice barely a whisper, "Don't believe everything you see. There can be deceptions. The desert casts illusions that can trick the mind."

Elara sang the lovely melody of the tribal song in her tent as the night's soft humming blended with her tribal song. However, the peace appeared to alter, indicating the course the team was about to take.

Once a representation of everlasting beauty, the golden dunes harbored deception and illusions as dawn broke, suggesting the difficult journey ahead. It was not easy to search for the Manifesto.

The line separating fact from mirage would become increasingly hazy, putting their unity and views of reality to the test. Not only would the Hades Manifesto be revealed along the way, but history's shadows of betrayal would also be encountered.

Chapter Six: Mirage of Betrayal

The desert's wide area was misleading. What looked like a short distance could be kilometers of sand dunes with curves. Carter covered his eyes and squinted to determine if the faraway shape was a figment of his imagination or reality playing tricks on him in the shimmering heat. The desert stretches one's memory and makes it play out like a movie reel. His pulse pounded briefly as he believed he recognized a face from his past. Still, the shadow immediately disappeared with the winds that were blowing wildly.

Alice was right behind Carter. She knelt behind him, her fingertips tracing the golden sands. Her historian's instincts sensitively felt the layers of stories buried beneath each grain.

"This land has memories. Not just ours, but generations gone by," she muttered. She turned to face Amina, looking for a sign of reassurance or validation.

Amina's black eyes were hard to read as she grinned slightly. She replied to Alice cryptically, "Those who listen, the desert communicates. But not all voices are well-intentioned, so one must be cautious about what they hear."

Kofi was quick to hear that. He had already begun establishing a perimeter to ensure the safety of their brief halt. Elara started playing a mellow, almost haunting tune as she tried to contact the rhythm of the desert after feeling the tension in the air. Due to the delicate, melancholy sounds, the dunes' spirits appeared to stir in response to her appeal.

But the group was increasingly plagued by Carter's diversion. He was becoming affected by the desert's illusions, making it difficult to distinguish between truth, recollection, conviction, and psychosis. Every swaying shadow and wind whisper had a darker, more threatening meaning. His former trust was now tinted with skepticism, and he noticed he was always looking at Amina. Was she going to save them from this ruthless wilderness, or was she just giving them false hopes?

The desert seemed to come to life as Elara's music continued, its emptiness resonating with the whispers of those who had passed away. Sensing the atmosphere, Amina started speaking in her rhythmic, appealing voice.

"While the sands vary, the stories stay. It has heard confessions of love, betrayal, hope, and sorrow. It has watched kingdoms grow and fall."

Alice was extremely interested as she listened carefully.

"Are there legends particular to these places that talk about the Hades Manifesto?" She asked.

"Some legends about a relic with great power have been passed down through the decades. Still, these legends also contain warnings of trickery and mirages that mislead seekers." Amina added.

In the meantime, Kofi rejoined the group and faintly indicated to Carter that he had noticed a group of figures with unknown intents on the horizon. The scavenger's instincts were quite active. Carter interpreted this as further evidence of his doubts because his thinking was already clouded with uncertainty. Were they being led into a trap by Amina? Could they trust her?

Elara shifted her tone delicately as she became more nervous. A more upbeat tune was intended to promote group unity and clarity in their minds. But the illusions of the desert were growing more robust, and the distinction between friend and foe was becoming a bit hard to trace.

Alice started reading aloud from an antique scroll she had just discovered amid the menacing mirages. The sentences flowed like poetry, and the script was complex. They claimed that the desert's defense against those unworthy of its riches was provided by its mirages. These deceptions did prey upon the fears and wants of the people, either leading them off track or on track.

Kofi's hand moved for his dagger, which was a result of his reflex action. As the figures on the horizon got closer, they flickered as strong for one second and as friendly traders the next. Were they threatening, or were they just mirages created by the desert?

Carter was closely watching Amina. In these difficult moments, her composed calmness seemed weird.

He yelled, "How do you suggest we go through these illusions?"

"By placing your trust in the realities of your heart rather than the lies of your eyes," Amina said with a grin.

Seeing an opportunity, Elara began to play a quiet, thoughtful song. The notes were screaming out in the middle of the delusions, trying to connect with something genuine. As she continued to play, the wind carried an answer in the form of an eerie tune that drew them even further into the desert.

Amid the deceptions that were so confusing to them, the distant melody woven into Elara's song offered the group a feeling of direction. A route that was lighted by the setting sun, suddenly appeared as the notes drifted through the dry desert air. But this path was made of sound and feeling—a guiding resonance—rather than sand or stone.

Carter's attention was still on Amina as the harmony awe-struck the rest of the group.

"Who is playing that tune? Tell me, who is it?" He asked with mistrust in his voice.

Amina pointed to the immense desert that was all about them.

"Carter, one only needs to listen, as the desert has so much to say to all of you," Amina said.

Alice suddenly made the connection while looking very thoughtful. As they went, directed by the tune, those mirages totally disappeared.

"The scroll," she shouted, "is like referencing the desert guiding those considered worthy with its song. This is what it meant. Wow, I finally see it."

But when the illusions vanished, the anxiety increased. The team could now see the torchlights of an approaching caravan in the clarity of the night. Were they friends or enemies? Could they be trusted at all?

The area was lit up by those torches, which were starkly contrasting with the sky filled with stars. Kofi, constantly on the lookout, examined the horizon and noticed several people coming their way with great haste. Their silhouette did not indicate their identities or motives, which made the approaching conflict even more mysterious.

"Why would anyone walk the desert at night other than us?" Alice muttered, her voice was full of curiosity and concern.

Elara played instinctually as if to comfort or speak with the far-off people.

Amina took deep breaths. Her enigmatic words hung in the air, increasing doubt, "The desert conceals many, Alice. Some search for lost souls, some look for treasures, while others only mirror our greatest fears."

Carter spoke about the open ground's perils as he clenched his dagger's hilt. He had learned to be wary of shocks in the past, especially when they occurred at night. However, as the team readied themselves for this confrontation, it quickly became apparent that it would be unlike any other, testing their physical prowess, sense of reality, and trust.

The shadows of all the far-off people grew longer. They moved with uneven steps as they drew nearer, interweaving to form a captivating sight on the dunes. It was hard to tell what was genuine and what was an illusion because of how the torches they held up looked to pulse. As the figures finally reached the center of the dunes, their purpose became clear. Their torches cast long, dancing shadows on the sand. The onlookers held their breath, captivated by the mesmerizing display unfolding before them.

Alice, always an academic, was fascinated by its beauty and mystique.

She said, "Desert light phenomena, yeah, that's what it is," recalling ancient texts she had read about hallucinations that could be heard and felt as much as seen. Or something much older and sentient, she considered as a chill suddenly crept down her spine.

Elara's once serene and lovely melody took on an eerie tune, which mirrored the tension that was so obvious in the atmosphere. Sensing the change, Kofi took a defensive posture between the group and the moving strangers, which wasn't lost on Alice. In that instant, the bond they shared in silence was a lot stronger.

Maintaining her composed demeanor, Amina advanced as the tension slowly escalated amongst the group. She spoke firmly, "These are the guardians of the Mirage. They stand as sentinels over the desert's secrets and illusions, for they neither bring harm nor help. The group exchanged puzzled looks as Amina's declaration carried the weight of legendary tales. In his constant vigilance, Carter moved closer to Alice, protecting her just a little, and placed her behind him.

The Guardians' leader, a towering man dressed in flowing robes of the desert that reflected the colors of the sky, moved forward. He measured and weighed each person in the group with eyes that were hidden by an elaborate mask. His voice was like the desert wind, whispering, yet impossible to grasp: "Why do you invade the regions of the Mirage?"

Alice took a step forward after gathering her bravery. She said, her voice echoing with the weight of her mission, "We seek the Hades Manifesto." The Guardians murmured as she said those words; their previously indifferent demeanor was now marked by apparent unease.

As she hovered over her instrument, Elara started playing a haunting melody that vibrated with the sand. The music was intended to promote trust and calmness—a bridge between worlds and intentions—and was influenced by old desert lullabies she had once heard.

The sands appeared to hum in unison as Elara's song filled the space with its mystical melodies. Kofi, who had always trusted his senses, closed his eyes, and let the music wash over him as he listened for any danger or wicked intent.

Carter couldn't shake the unease that had settled in his gut. As he observed Amina, his gaze fixed on her lips, which perfectly harmonized with the haunting melody that filled the air. It was as if she were whispering hidden secrets to the wind, creating an invisible lullaby that mixed with the enthralling music. Carter knew that he couldn't let his guard down. There were truths and tricks hidden beneath the shifting sands of the desert.

Murmurs were silenced by the Guardians' leader raising a hand. He began to address the group, "The Manifesto is not simply a story or a treasure to be discovered. It is the lifeblood of our past, our legacy. The sands have taught us that you come here as seekers, not conquerors."

"We don't want to take the Manifesto; we just only want to understand it. The secrets it holds can change the fate of many people." Alice replied, clutching the ancient map tightly in her hands. Her sincere plea struck a chord, but the tension in the air remained.

Amina moved closer to the Guardians' leader, giving him a polite nod as she held out her hand to expose a tiny vial of glowing sand. The sparkling grains moved on their own, generating symbols and patterns that changed and danced constantly.

Her voice was soothing as she said, "The desert sees all and forgets nothing. These sands remember the footprints of people who walked here ages ago and whisper secrets to those who know how to listen."

Kofi experienced an odd association with the vial. He could hear the whispering of the sands inside, which were loud in his ears. He whispered to Alice, "We're on the right track," and she nodded in agreement.

Carter, on the other hand, was more resistant to most things in his life. His suspicion increased even though he understood the ritual's significance and the respect it demanded. Carter said, "Symbols in the sand won't protect us from genuine threats." But Elara, who was standing close by, said, "Sometimes, Carter, it's the intangible that holds the most power," gently touching his arm. A delicate tune flowed from her lips, echoing the emotion, adding another layer to the already-growing mystery.

The atmosphere created by Elara's gentle hum enveloped the group in a ghostly bubble as it mingled with the breeze. The dread that had crept into their hearts was mirrored in the air, which appeared thicker with tension. Elara's tune drew Alice in, and she started to hum along, bringing forth an ancient tongue that appeared to interconnect with the changing sands.

Elara and Alice performed an impromptu dance while keeping their eyes closed, their feet creating patterns on the ground that matched the symbols in the sand of the vial. The air fizzed with something that infused them, casting a spell that ensnared the bunch. The Guardians marveled as they saw an ancient ritual with which they were familiar.

A change in the wind caused Kofi to experience a chill down his spine. His instincts for defense heightened as he rubbed his palms. He approached the pair, prepared to step in if necessary. Carter's mistrust grew throughout, even though he could feel the electricity around them.

As enthralled as they were, none of them paid attention to the shadowy figures lurking around the edges of their campground. They watched the ritual, their eyes shining in the dusk, waiting for the right time to announce their presence.

The surrounding dunes appeared to ripple and tremble as the music became more intense. It was as if they were mirroring the sad melody. Amina's eyes ran to the receding sands as her gaze sharpened. The swaying of the dunes was caused by something that was much more mysterious than the wind.

Raheem, the Guardian, stood with his staff raised high. The crystal embedded in it was gleaming in the fading light. He spoke in a faint voice, "The sands can talk. They are whispering tales of treachery, friends becoming enemies, and about antagonists."

Still lost in her trance, Elara made a discordant sound with her melody. With a mixture of caution and intrigue, Alice said something incomprehensible. The designs they had painted on the ground started transforming into symbols nobody else recognized except Amina.

Carter went for the leather pouch by his side as his fingertips brushed the cool metal of his concealed weapon because he could not stand still in the face of danger. However, Kofi was the one to make the initial move. He prepared to guard against the betrayal the sands had warned him about by positioning himself between the captivated pair and the approaching danger with his sword in his hand.

A sudden windstorm whisked the sand grains, revealing a vast, intricately carved stone door beneath them. Its surface was covered in inscriptions that were lost. No, it wasn't a mirage; it served as a portal, leading directly to the historical records they sought.

Kofi growled slowly; it was like a warning as he became aware of the tense situation. Once more, the sand beneath their feet moved, and ancient guards with lifelike stone bodies and blue-lit eyes appeared alive. With their weapons, they crowded the crew.

"The Desolation Guardians, keepers of ages-old truths," Amina mumbled to herself.

Carter nodded a little as he looked at Alice. They knew they had experienced being outnumbered and surrounded when he was in the military. Remembering her previous experiences, Alice repeated a series of incantations she had learned throughout her studies to appease the Guardians.

Carter pulled out a small, metallic device and turned it on at the same time. The heavens were lit up by a brilliant flare that rocketed upward. The guards paused, their stone bodies blinking despite the artificial lighting. Taking advantage of the opportunity, Kofi and

Carter launched a synchronized attack that forced the guardians back and opened the big door.

Their efforts were assisted by the melodies created by Elara's fingers on her instrument. It weaved protection and power into the air. There was a furious struggle of intelligence, power, and cunning. The combined strength of Carter and Alice was unbeatable – as it was developed through countless battles, it ensured the guardians were kept at bay.

The stone door rumbled and started to open as the last of the guardians moved away. A surge of chilly air struck them, revealing a beckoning blackness. The entrance to an underground labyrinth that they had discovered had the promise of becoming the key to the Hades Manifesto. However, they knew this was only the start of their struggles. Although the draw of what lay beyond was strong, they were also aware that the distinction between reality and a mirage, friend, and adversary, would become even more hazy as they moved forward.

The labyrinth walls seemed to pulse with an old vitality as they descended. A language older than anyone they knew illuminated the path sporadically with blue, glowing symbols. Their erratic shadow movements gave the impression that someone was watching them from just outside the light. There was an eerie feeling in the air that made the air itself thick with anticipation.

"Stay united because it is rumored that the labyrinth shifts and changes, fooling those who walk inside," Amina murmured in a hushed voice that reverberated through the stone hallways.

Carter and Alice sensed an unsettling familiarity as they continued along the hallways as if they had been here before. They talked inaudibly while pointing out potential traps, ambush locations, and escape routes as their military senses were heightened.

The labyrinth's walls abruptly began to move. Pathways started to disappear, while others appeared due to the friction between the stones. This was more than just a maze; it was a living, breathing thing that appeared determined to trap them.

Ethereal voices emerged from the depths and started to chant, creating illusions. Their eyesight was obscured by ghosts of former rivals, long-gone allies, and visions of nefarious betrayals. The notes of Elara's music became a lifeline to cling to as it served as a beacon of realism amidst the commotion.

Amina admitted inconsolably that the labyrinth doesn't simply test the body; it also torments the soul.

The training of Alice and Carter now went into overdrive. They guided the group, dodging traps, and phantom threats thanks to their shared recollection of previous operations. Their coordinated movements resembled a finely tuned performance, refined through countless years of working together in the field. They eventually came upon a complex painting featuring battle scenes and astonishingly included their faces among the old warriors. How did this happen?

Time doesn't go linearly here; the past, present, and future coexist, Kofi whispered, caressing the painting.

The significance of their mission was altered by this realization. They were constantly battling, not just the here and now.

Their faces could be seen among the ancient warriors, yet the mural continued. As it went on, scenes of their trek through the desert, their run-ins with illusions, and Amina leading them were revealed. But the subsequent visions of future events showed shadows with evil eyes following their every move.

Carter scrutinized the mural while chiseling away at the stone with the knife's edge. He looked at Alice, understanding the flow between them, "This isn't just painted on. It's entrenched into the walls, like a prophecy."

Alice muttered; we can't let anything divert us because we are a part of something greater.

A trap door under them suddenly opened, sending the group tumbling into a colossal chamber below. Carter and Alice quickly recovered to be surrounded by dark beings with evil-looking eyes.

Although Amina's advice had been significant, they now had to rely solely on their inherent talent. Sword clashes, battle screams, and Elara's reassuring harmonies resounded throughout the chamber.

Alice's blade swirled in the low light; her movements as smooth as water. Carter was an unstoppable force next to her, delivering each punch and kick with military precision. They united to build a powerful front that resisted the attack of shadows.

They didn't know the threat existed until Amina panicked. One of the shadows held a parchment with a remarkably similar design. The Hades Declaration. Yet how? They were expected to discover it first.

The crew was left gasping, resting, but unified as Elara, plucking her lyre with urgency, sang a tune that released dazzling light, causing the shadows to flee and scatter.

The Manifesto had vanished by the time the smoke cleared. But it was obvious that the secrets of the Manifesto were being protected by the shadows, who weren't just watching over the maze.

The gentle, eerie hum of a tune broke the stillness of the battle's aftermath. The squad only managed to catch their breath before turning to the source of the overwhelming tension in the air. In the center of where they were, a large lyre made of bones and adorned with symbols was perched upon a stone pedestal. Its strings began to quiver with each hum, creating an ethereal melody.

"This... it connects with the same energy as mine, but it's older, more... powerful," Elara said as she approached, her hands slightly trembling.

Carter and Alice looked at each other. Do you believe it could help us in our search? Carter asked.

Elara skillfully pulled on a cord. The note reverberated around the place, exposing wall carvings that had previously been obscured. She said, "Rhythms," as she traced the old writing with her fingertips. "This lyre can reveal the patterns concealed in the Hades Manifesto and the truth."

As she played, the floor shook, and the chamber's walls appeared to move, revealing a previously unnoticed corridor.

The tunnel was lined with symbols that individually lit up and pulsed in rhythm with the lyre's tune, unlike the previous maze.

Amina gestured toward the pathway while maintaining a cautious yet determined expression. The Manifesto isn't simply a paper; it's a symphony, a collection of rhythms, and to grasp it, we must comprehend its music.

Elara's new lyre and strange rhythms guided the party as they bravely entered the lighted tunnel. As they descended more, they realized how difficult their assignment was. They weren't merely lost in a maze but at the center of a harmonious musical puzzle where truth and deception played off one another.

Chapter Seven: Rhythms of Truth

Elara was quiet as her fingers danced over the lyre's strings as the party reassembled behind the cover of a giant palm tree. She liked the hauntingly lovely music that started to play, resonating strangely across the Oasis. Everyone's senses were heightened as they sat spellbound, enjoying the music.

Tamir whispered something in a dialect that most people in the group had never heard while his eyes were closed, and his head was slightly lowered to the ground. When Alice felt a sudden warmth in her hand, she opened her eyes, only to find that the compass she'd been handed began to glow and spin in a weird pattern or something... Amina glanced over at the compass right at the same time, appearing to be taken to another time and location.

Carter and Kofi exchanged curious glances as they understood the situation had shifted without warning. A previously unseen elaborate archway carved into a stone cliffside caught the group's attention. The arch's borders started to shimmer, and the interior area appeared to warp, which was a portal to another world.

Elara paused the music for a while; her voice started to quiver, and her face turned pale. "This song has been passed down through the centuries in my family, but I was unaware of its significance. It is really like a key and a portal."

The archway's glittering grew stronger as she finished speaking, displaying an old painting. It looked like some desert tribespeople, an instrument resembling Elara's lyre, and mysterious symbols encircling an image the group could identify with—a representation of the Hades Manifesto. They would delve even farther into the mysteries of the Oasis, whose past was like the tale of their mission.

The air became thick with expectancy as the group neared the painting. Tamir started chanting in the same dialect, keeping up with the beat of Elara's song while he traced the old symbols with his fingers. Each character appeared to come to life and emit a faint glow upon his touch.

"I've seen these symbols in a dream... or a memory. They tell a narrative hidden away in my lineage," Amina murmured faintly as Carter broke her trance.

As she talked, a section of the artwork moved, exposing a hollow area. It contained an old instrument with a shape resembling Elara's lyre and embroidered with rich metals and stones. The Oasis began to ring as soon as Elara's fingers touched it. The sound was a perfect harmony connecting the past and present.

A sudden blast of wind spun the sand about them, and a tall, imposing figure emerged from the whirling vortex. He identified himself as Nazir while wearing traditional desert garb that only revealed his piercing eyes via a veil. "Defender of truths," he proclaimed. "The time has arrived to reveal the wisdom you seek, but first, you must demonstrate your value. I have waited for the chosen ones for so long, it seems like ages."

To Nazir's remarks, the Oasis appeared to react. The shifting sands revealed obstacles and riddles, previewing the team's difficulties. Even though their quest was far from complete, the appearance of the desert guardian gave them renewed hope and the courage to face reality's rhythm.

Alice looked narrowly at Nazir. Her military inclinations were on high alert. She asked, her palm resting on the hilt of her blade, "How can we trust you?

Nazir only grinned, but his smile fell short of his eyes. He cryptically responded, "Trust is a decision, just like betrayal is. However, The Oasis's decision to show itself to you should mean something."

Kofi moved forward, his eyes reflecting the mural's patterns. He declared firmly, remembering a similar design he'd seen in a temple from his country of origin, "We're here seeking answers, not riddles.

Elara played the instrument she had just found, creating a sad song. In response, the Oasis revealed a walkway made of steppingstones that led to an underground chamber. The identical symbols from the painting were well-lit on each stone.

Carter examined the first stone after becoming curious.

"It looks like a series," he said quietly.

He remembered a strikingly similar strategic training exercise from his military days: "Each stone has to be activated in a certain order, like a pattern of some sort."

"The route is there, but only those with pure hearts and unclouded intentions can traverse it; one slip-up can endanger everyone," Nazir said and nodded in agreement.

The group shared meaningful glances with each other right that moment. They were unified in their determination and started to decode the rhythmic pattern, each member bringing their own specialization to the puzzle as it came together. They knew that a significant revelation was about to occur, but the journey through the rhythms of truth had only begun.

The more Elara played, the more intense it became. A corresponding stone lit up in response to each note. With her tactical expertise, Alice took the initiative and carefully stepped on each rock in time with Elara's music. To ensure that everyone moved in unison, the crew followed her as she moved.

When Alice was ready to step onto the penultimate stone, a sudden wind from the Oasis threw sand into her eyes, causing her to stumble. The rock beneath her suddenly darkened, and the ground shook, spreading waves across the Oasis's waters.

Nazir raised his voice, declaring, "The Oasis is challenging your determination; you must press on and deepen your resolve."

Carter moved forward quickly and grabbed Alice's arm. He yanked her onto the stone to light the way again. The trembling stopped as abruptly as it had started.

Realizing they had come close to tragedy, the team felt relieved. The pathway continued behind them, but up ahead was a stone door with symbols that matched those on the mural and the stones, which was the starting point for their search for solutions.

Kofi said, "We are getting near now," as he pushed closer to Alice. "Your senses have saved us."

The team gathered before the door to prepare for what lay beyond. For the first time, Nazir gazed at them with sincere compassion. "Brace yourselves; some may find truths beyond this door challenging to accept." he said, smiling at them.

Kofi closely examined the symbols on the stone door and realized they weren't just for show; they possessed more than just aesthetics. He could see them moving in time with Elara's music, shifting and realigning. Elara felt this dance of symbols was encouraging her to perform a certain melody.

Elara began to nervously strum her instrument, "I think this door demands a special song to open, one that's ancient and almost forgotten with time. I think I can do it." Each chord she played caused a slight movement in the door.

Raif, who was a historian and linguist, suddenly moved forward from the group and said to them, "The song of the desert tribes, which is thought to be the key to their most prized secrets, is represented by these symbols, which speak of a legend that I have once read."

Elara immediately recognized the sad melody he was softly humming. She was quick to copy those notes on her instrument. As the melodies filled the air, a subtle tremor ran through the ground beneath them, echoing the vibrations of the stone door. It was as if the music itself held the key to unlocking the ancient passage. However, the tune was abruptly interrupted by a robust and dissonant note, which briefly caused the door to become immobile. Alice turned to look around as her intuition took over. A man concealed beneath a desert cloak stepped out from the darkness. They were obviously not alone in their search. There was someone with them, someone who had just made himself known.

Elara turned to the group while clearly shaken. They stood protectively around her, ready to meet any challenge this new player brought.

"We need to finish the song. We can't let him interrupt us with that." She said in a quivering tone.

She knew what she had to do. She began singing with courage, the notes echoing off the walls and filling the room with beautiful harmonies as the cloaked figure stepped forward with assurance. A unique piece of jewelry on the intruder's neck caught Carter's attention. It was a half-crescent moon enclosing a desert rose, signifying an ancient desert clan.

This trespasser wasn't just any trespasser; they really had extensive knowledge and connections to the past.

After a moment of deep thinking, Kofi signaled Alice. Alice moved softly in a circle to the stranger's side with a smoothness that belied their shared history and trust. However, the intruder interrupted her as she was about to move, speaking in a low, gravelly whisper. "The Manifesto is not what you think it is, and I'm not here to hurt anyone but to help. Trust me with this. I know what I am saying."

Raif moved closer as his eyes widened in recognition. He whispered, "Zafar?"

When Zafar removed his hood, his aged and sun-damaged face was visible. "Raif, oh my, it's been a while," he said, looking at Elara.

The Manifesto's secrets are more than just information; they also contain a force. You must finish the song but with caution."

The team prepared themselves for the possibility that opening this door could drastically alter everything as they were now engulfed in the mysterious aura of the Oasis.

The room fell silent as Zafar and Raif's eyes met, two ancient souls meeting after eons apart. The air appeared rich with history, with long-buried memories emerging. Seeing the significance of the situation, Elara began to play a gentle, melodic song about lost connections and ties that even the passage of time couldn't break.

Carter couldn't help but question Zafar, "Why are you here, and how do you know of the manifesto? I thought it was just us."

Zafar took a deep breath and said, "I've come to lead, not to make problems for you all. Like Elara's, my ancestry is connected to the desert tribes, the guardians of the Manifesto's secrets. Over the years, so many stories have hidden its actual nature. It's not a thing, but a profound knowledge."

Despite her skepticism, Alice sensed Zafar's sincerity when he said those words. Elara, though, moved first as her senses led her. "Then, show us that time is not a luxury we can afford."

"The journey is risky, but with each other's help, we can win this. We just need to stick with each other," Zafar said.

The group united under Zafar's guidance and began to trust them. Their mission's mystery intensified, but they grew more determined with each added piece of information. The team was prepared to accept whatever lay ahead because the Hunt for the Hades Manifesto was becoming a journey of self-discovery for all of them.

Zafar started spinning a tale in the faint light of the room, transporting everyone to a bygone era. Kofi instantly recognized the patterns and understood that this was more than a story because of his keen thinking. This was a mysterious map.

According to Zafar, who spoke with trembling intensity, one can only hear and feel the rhythms of the truth if they are at peace with themselves and the environment. "There's an oasis buried deep within the desert, known only to a few."

Alice mumbled, "The Dance of the Spirits. I remember my grandma often talked about it. It's like a ceremony of the desert tribes to connect with the ancient spirits," her fingertips brushing the old pendant her grandmother once wore.

Zafar looked at her with understanding in his eyes. "The dancing is the secret, and the Oasis is real. Absolutely real."

"We'll need supplies and a guide to navigate the desert because the circumstances can be harsh," said Dahlia in a practical tone.

Zafar said, "I can guide you, but be ready—the desert requires more than physical strength. A lot more than just that."

The team started preparing after Zafar provided some much-needed clarification. Each team member contributes, and each talent stands out. Although the mystery strengthened, they were even more determined to find the Hades Manifesto and the secrets that could help them with their self-discovery.

As a team, they were really focused on starting this leg of their mission as dawn well-lit the desert in shades of orange and gold. Zafar had been able to assemble camels for the trek, guaranteeing they would move quickly across the sands. Kofi had an in-depth discussion with Zafar, interpreting the hidden implications in the story of the Oasis using his skill of understanding most of the ancient languages.

Dahlia was busy setting up a temporary camp for everybody while Alice honed her extensive survival skills while performing the Dance of the Spirits. She had found a nearby well, but the water they pulled was murky, dense, and black.

Dahlia shouted, "Wait! The water is contaminated."

Alice came over with a purifying device she had prepared for times like these. "We can distill this," she said with assurance.

Kofi discovered several desert plants while digging through the sand. "Tribes utilize these to purify tainted supplies. Thus, they can be helpful as well." He told everyone with a polite gesture.

They quickly put a structure in place thanks to Kofi's adaptability to change so quickly, Alice's understanding, and Dahlia's practical talents. It really meant a lot to them. With their combined expertise, the previously impure water was purified and rendered clear for drinking.

With the newfound trust growing amid them, they confronted the obstacles with an intensified focus, delving even deeper into the desert's mysteries, bound by their shared vision in their relentless pursuit. With the camels swinging, the gentle whispering sands, and the group's shared steady hum of determination, they journeyed deeper into the desert and took on a rhythm. Dahlia carefully observed their water consumption, making sure that they drank enough to stay hydrated without wasting any water.

Alice observed a strange pattern in the sand on the third day. She drew the group's attention to the lines and traced them to show an elaborate but old map.

Kofi considered, his gaze more focused, "This isn't just a natural formation."

Zafar knelt next to it and touched the surface lightly with his fingers. "We are close to the Manuscript's last resting place, yet the sands conceal stories."

But as Alice performed the Dance of Spirits over the map, she unintentionally sparked a sandstorm, the furious guardian of the desert. Their visions blurred as the howling winds threatened to destroy them.

Kofi recommended they form a circle and grab onto each other, camels, and all, as he recalled stories of similar storms. The group trusted his instincts and used the circle as a haven from the tumult. The map was lost after the storm passed, but their course appeared more evident than ever. "Onward," Dahlia said, as she turned to face the horizon.

"The desert tests people, but it also directs. So, we need to follow the directions."

The group moved forward with newfound resolve after having a close encounter with the fury of the desert. A previously hidden route of smooth stones embedded in the sand was now visible because of the calm breezes. These stones guided their path with a gentle brightness that resembled ancient stars that had fallen from the sky.

Zafar immediately recognized the stones as the "Lanterns of Lore" due to his proficiency in ancient cultures. He said, "A guardian tribe set these for us to realize that we are on the way to hallowed knowledge."

With her spiritual connection, Alice sensed a pull in one direction. She started to hum a song from her youth that she remembered. The stones reverberated with the music, making them shine even more radiantly.

Dahlia discovered pieces of an antique parchment right when they were still walking. Only Kofi was able to understand the script that was used to write it. "It alludes to a trial," he continued, "It's not enough to simply uncover the Manifesto; we also need to demonstrate that we are worthy of learning its secrets. We need to deserve to know about it."

Although the discovery was threatening, it simply made them more determined. Combining their skills and experience, they prepared for the difficulties ahead and moved closer to the hidden Hades Manifesto.

Dahlia experienced a sudden intuition as she followed the Lanterns of Lore's dazzling trail. "Do you understand that these stones are synchronizing with our wishes and illuminating our route," she asked after pausing for a bit.

Lena closely examined a stone with what she knew about science: "They react bioluminescent to our presence, making them appear alive and sensitive."

Zafar rubbed his brow in contemplation. "The prehistoric cultures thought that intention was a natural power, like the wind or water."

"Their memories of Alice's singing rekindled this ancient path's sensitivity," Kofi speculated, "Perhaps the actual test is not merely physical or mental, but of our fundamental intentions and togetherness," remembering the fragment's mention of a trial.

Their hypothesis was quickly put to the test. The light path split into two separate directions. But instead of disagreement or perplexity, they all experienced a robust internal tug to the left.

Their faith in one another and the journey soon paid off. A historic amphitheater filled with ghostly echoes could be seen at the end of the meandering path. They were working together to find the Hades Manifesto when they discovered the following clue.

The group observed a plinth with an odd relic in the middle of the amphitheater. It was a mask, with one half made of obsidian and the other appearing to be made of the most transparent crystal. First to arrive, Zafar thought, "This might be a symbolic portrayal of the balance between knowledge and the unknown" due to his historical understanding.

A beautiful, lilting melody began to play when Dahlia touched the crystal side of the mask, filling the room with its melancholy sounds. The melody held an eerie blend of familiarity and distant echoes. Alice had earlier hummed the same tune.

Kofi, who has a natural affinity for music, started to move to the beat. His motions caused reverberations in the air, and when the others joined him, the amphitheater was filled with a symphony of rhythmic movement. They danced as a single organism, not individuals, bound together by their search and the rhythm of truth.

Alice was the one who noticed a vague vibration under her feet as she was dancing. She squatted down and found a secret compartment. A paper with burnt edges and precise information was within; it detailed a celestial map and the next section of their voyage.

Their dance had been a cause for celebration and the solution. The next phase in unlocking the secrets of the Hades Manifesto had been revealed by the harmony of their spirits and the antiquated rhythms. They had encountered a difficulty, remained steadfast in their commitment, and triumphed again.

The team's attention was drawn to the celestial map Alice was holding as it began to gently shimmer. A complex trail leading to a vast desert, famed in tales as the place where the past whispered to the present, was revealed as the stars and constellations rearranged.

Dahlia mumbled, "Incredible. It is more than just a map; it is a tangible reminder of our journey.

Zafar traced a particularly brilliant star cluster with his fingers while squinting. "I've read this pattern represents the Oasis of Echoes, where time follows no rules."

They were led to their next location by the melody they danced to, echoing indistinctly in the distance. A pocket compass Kofi always carried with him felt heavy. Now that it was tuned in to the rhythms they discovered, it was swaying towards the direction of the Oasis.

Her eyes glued to the horizon Alice thought, "This trek is a monument to our stubbornness. Every misstep is merely a steppingstone to a revelation."

When they reached the edges of the desert, where the sands were shifting with stories from the past, their steps started coordinating with the underlying rhythm of the earth. The Oasis of Echoes awaited them as they entered, promising secrets concealed beyond its ethereal cloak. Each grain of sand had a piece of an old story that signaled to be recounted, and our crew felt the draw of stories and the charm of mysteries that remained unanswered.

The usual heat breathed life into their surroundings as they traveled further into the desert. Ahead, figures that resembled mirages danced, fusing reality and fantasy. But amid this, a significant impediment appeared: a sandstorm blocking their way to the Oasis of Echoes.

"We must trust the resources we have been given and the rhythm we have found," Kofi shouted over the roaring sands as he felt his compass pull in a magnetic direction.

Alice started humming the tune, which had now become their north star, remembering their prior experience. As she was humming, Zafar reached into his backpack and brought out a silver flute, whose melody joined hers in a charming duet.

In response to the music, the whirling sands started to move, clearing a path through the storm. Dahlia danced along this path, guiding the group, and scattering the hostile elements as she recalled her knowledge of ancient desert rituals.

The group discovered themselves at the edge of a tranquil oasis as the storm's final traces vanished. The celestial map was reflected in the calm waters, hinting at the secrets the Oasis contained.

Stories from the past seemed to drift on the breeze in whispers. There was no doubt that they were about to make a significant discovery. The team was able to successfully overcome the desert's difficulty and obstacles. The sands slowly shifted; they whispered of more profound mysteries yet to be unraveled.

Chapter Eight: Shifting Sands

The desert sun scorched everything in the area, creating airy mirages of long-gone towns that spread across the horizon. He stood against the golden dunes as Maxwell emerged from the vast territory's heat waves. He had devoted his life to exploring lost cultures and solving their riddles. He was raised in Cairo's bustling streets and trained under the close supervision of some of the country's top archaeologists.

Maxwell's greatest accomplishment was discovering artifacts from Heraklion. This lost city had been submerged for more than a thousand years. Maxwell had made a name for himself as a leading archaeologist with a keen eye for detail and the essence of historical trends. He was adept at establishing connections where others failed. He was renowned for having a remarkable gift for understanding ancient texts, making him a priceless resource in the hunt for the abstract Hades Manifesto.

Sophia contacted Maxwell because of his unmatched expertise in ancient city blueprints, particularly those buried beneath desert sands. Maxwell asserted that the Hades Manifesto belonged to his great-grandfather before Bedouins stole it; as a result, Maxwell's most recent work, joining the team, was personal.

In addition to restoring his family's name, Maxwell was now dedicated to ensuring that the knowledge contained in the Manifesto profited everyone.

The Hades Manifesto was hidden among these ruins, waiting to be discovered as they stood on the edge of history. The crew froze, taking in the immensity of their discoveries as one member squinted, using his hand as a shade, and whispered, "Civilizations lost to time."

Under the intense light, the vast desert looked like a sea of golden waves. With each step, the team's feet dug deeper into the warm sand. Jade was distrustful that they weren't alone, so she watched their surroundings. Serena was the first to see the towering structure up ahead, hidden by the sloping dunes. "Over there," she yelled, pointing to a deserted area of a former city.

The group quickened their pace with a fresh enthusiasm, their steps displaying anticipation. But the immensity of the desert was misleading. The journey to the ruins took hours, far longer than anyone had anticipated.

Given his understanding of other civilizations, Maxwell deduced, "This could be the remnants of the vanished city of Zaratha. If my studies serve me right, it was once a bustling hub of knowledge and commerce."

Ethan said, "Imagine the secrets it could contain, perhaps even hints as to where the manifesto is located."

With a keen interest in putting her language skills to use, Serena began to search for all the inscriptions or symbols that might hold valuable information. "I might be able to understand the ancient texts in these structures, so let's spread out and start looking."

But a strange silence settled over the area when they approached the ruins. There was nothing but the soft rustling of sand in the desert breezes. The hush, though, was brief. From behind them, there was a low, gloomy hum. The uproar got louder and lasted longer.

"Sandstorm! It's coming our way rapidly," Jade shouted with an urgent tone!

"We have to find shelter." Ethan gave the order to immediately enter the ruins.

To escape the cruelty of the imminent desert storm, the team ran straight for the ruins. The mystery of the old city would have to wait. Staying alive was more important now.

As the winds strengthened and their visions progressively blurred, the ancient city offered sanctuary from the unrelenting storm. Narrow passageways and open chambers inside revealed the secrets of a bygone era. Using a handmade torch, Jade guided the group through a web of intricately carved walls that told tales of fearless warriors and epic journeys. Hearing the outside storm was a continual reminder of the threat still in the desert.

"Is everyone okay?" Alice inquired as she scanned her crew.

"All good here," Maxwell responded, gazing at the designs on a wall nearby.

Ethan remarked, "We need to gather ourselves and wait this out since the storm could go on for hours."

Jade glanced at him briefly, appreciation in her eyes. Ethan has been a member of the group since the start of their mission. The Hades Manifesto's potential impact on contemporary archaeology had him join them on their journey to Cairo. He quickly became a crucial team member due to his strategic thinking and ability to remain calm under pressure.

Ethan had already explained to them how he had spent his formative years poring over ancient atlases and trip diaries. He announced, "I live for the rush of discovery and the search of the unexplored."

In the ancient remains of Zaratha, he was at home. In his plan, Ethan stated, "Once the storm clears, we'll break into two teams: one will document and decipher, and the other will search for any fresh leads or potential dangers."

Maxwell nodded in agreement. There are a lot of mysteries that can be revealed in this city.

Despite the storm's relentless rage, inside the ruins, there was a sense of unity and purpose. Thanks to Ethan's strong leadership and spirit, the crew's eagerness to discover the secrets the ruins concealed had never been stronger. The echo of their words and the faint external rumblings created an eeric mood in the ruins. The dim light reflected from the candles they held gave the ancient writings on the stone walls a glittering appearance. None of them had ever witnessed the depictions of rites, ceremonies, or intricate dancing patterns.

Alice's fingertips traced the etched symbols as her mind instantly deciphered their underlying meanings. "The inscriptions suggest that this place may have been a sanctuary or an area of devotion since they speak of dancing to the gods to win their favor."

"Dance has always been a narrative, a bridge between realms, according to some of the older dance forms I've studied," said Jade, the team's expert in ancient arts and traditions.

Her knowledge was founded on her love of dance and its historical significance. When the team found itself in Istanbul and was trying to translate signs regarding ancient performance ceremonies, Jade's knowledge had proven to be essential. She had joined the hunt for the Hades Manifesto to interpret the old-fashioned dance forms and tales buried in the mists of time since she was the link between the past and the present.

"Dancing as directed would disclose something for us. A hidden room or tunnel," Jade continued, her eyes bright with knowledge.

Ethan expressed passion. "It's conceivable because these ancient cities are full of secrets and mechanisms hidden from our view."

Maxwell gestured to the elevated platform in the center of the room, its significance now clear. "I think we've found our stage. Jade, are you up to the challenge?"

Jade nodded, a determined expression on her face. "Always."

As Jade prepared for the ancient dance, the ruins around them remained silent. The team took a position to observe while holding a torch in each hand to cast a fluttering circle of light around the platform since they were fascinated and intrigued.

Alice quickly outlined the actions as Jade promptly went over the symbols. The movements were graceful and elegant, evoking a comparison to previous times. Jade began to move, following the rhythm of her breathing as she drew on her prior knowledge of comparable dance forms.

In the torchlight, her shadow danced on the walls, each step and swirl lending to the ruins a sinister look. As she ran faster, each stride consistent with a phrase or sentence from the texts, the symbols Alice deciphered came to life.

Ethan, Maxwell, and Alice observed the dance intently, slowly realizing its significance. The event was more than just a show; it was necessary. They could feel a notable change in the atmosphere that suggested the sands outside were taking notice of the dance's impact.

After what seemed like a lifetime, Jade finally stopped, her breathing tense and her brow beaded with sweat. But the ruins responded. Then, right before their eyes, a portion of the floor revealed a staircase leading further into the chambers. At the same time, a subtle rumble echoed through the entire area.

Mostly speaking to himself, Ethan said, "Doesn't the past have a way of coming back to haunt us?"

Maxwell countered, "Let's see where these leads. There's more to this desert than changing sands."

The entire team stopped at the mouth of the stairway and scrutinized down into the dim depths below. A torch from above could only partially break through the deep darkness, which seemed to last forever. It had no limits. Elara touched the ancient stone steps and bent down to trace the carved patterns with her fingers. She felt enthralled by the atmosphere and the stones in front of her.

The others waited while she closed her eyes for a while to take in the energy of the place since they respected her intuition. She opened her eyes with a determined look. She said, "I can sense the intensity of the Manifesto getting closer to us. These stairs have stories to tell."

"No matter how close it might be, we must be prepared for whatever lies below," said Carter as he double-checked his gear once again.

"We won't be going in blind," Kofi said, holding up and turning on a flashlight.

Alice nodded, thinking about any potential language barriers they could encounter. She spoke to Jade briefly as they mentally prepared for their roles in figuring out and even solving new puzzles.

Maxwell took over as leader and led the team cautiously, directing them where to step or grasp and displaying his expertise in archeological excavations as they began their downward journey. The temperature dropped as they continued to descend, and the silence of the ancient underground world surrounded them. Only sometimes did the sound of sand shifting above them or the distant echo of their footsteps remind them they were still on Earth.

Murals, inscriptions, and other ancient artifacts appeared on the nearby walls as they descended. They would soon have access to the mysteries of a long-buried city.

The paintings encircling the basement-like space were a brilliant dance of colors that drew the onlooker in even after what felt like ages. It wasn't simply art but a graphic history of a society that highly emphasized education. The team was compelled to learn more and explore the underground world further with each painting and inscription.

Alice placed her fingertips on the carved characters and read the writings. "These symbols resemble an ancient form of hieroglyphics, but they are subtle, strange, and challenging to translate," she mumbled to herself.

Elara approached a painting that attracted her attention since it depicted the sun setting behind a giant pyramid. She reasoned, "This is not simply history; this is a map. The setting sun may symbolize a specific direction or a point in time."

Carter took out his compass, trying to match their position with the mural's possible orientation. "We must move forth and westward," he declared.

"The artwork portrays intellectuals who are ostensibly guardians of the Manifesto." After looking at a separate wall, Maxwell remarked, "It speaks of a ceremonial ritual involving the Manifesto."

"The knowledge is being ceremoniously handed on from one guardian to the next." Jade was able to make connections right away.

Ethan nodded in agreement and added, "So, what you're saying is that our Manifesto is more than just a series of instructions or a treasure map; it's holy to this long-forgotten civilization."

The search for the Hades Manifesto was intensifying, and the weight of its importance could be felt. They heard the faintest of echoes and footsteps that didn't belong to any of the team members, which is when Kofi said, "We're not alone." Serena swiftly devised a strategy to deal with or escape whatever was after them.

A sudden gust of wind blew out their torches just as Carter was about to put them out. The group was thrown into total darkness. Carter focused his gaze on the dim light coming from the embers of their torches on a strange arrangement of symbols close to the chamber's entrance. These symbols stood out from the others, as a warning.

"We need to be ready," Kofi whispered, instinctively reaching for his tools to set up a temporary trap for unwanted guests, as the only sound that broke the tense calm was the distant sound of footsteps.

Elara detected a change in the area's energy since she was constantly aware of her surroundings. "They are not merely a maze; they are created to test the worthiness of those who seek the Manifesto," she reasoned of these halls.

Ethan, trying to summon the knowledge he acquired about ancient defense strategies, said, "If we follow the patterns on the floor, they might guide us to a safer route, avoiding any potential traps."

"Consider our goal. We have access to the Hades Manifesto. We cannot afford any uncertainties at this point." Serena gently reminded them; it was needed.

As Jade held Alice's arm for support in the dark room, she remembered a chant she had heard before about that was said to illuminate passageways in ancient rooms. As she continued reading the texts, a slight glow originated from specific floor tiles, lighting the path.

Maxwell said, "Using bioluminescent elements to guide the way. Remarkable! Amazing idea, really! The ancients were indeed geniuses."

They moved steadily as a team, the weight of their goal pressing heavily upon them. However, the glow on the ground functioned as a reminder that with each stride, they were closer to discovering the secrets of the Hades Manifesto.

As they progressed along the illuminated route, they entered a majestic hall that took their breath away. Massive pillars stretching upward and blending with the sky supported the ceiling. On either side of the room's spacious area, enormous statues of long-forgotten kings and queens stood, their eyes watching the guests in their land.

With his eyes narrowing, Kofi said, "This place... it's not just a testament to history, but an assertion of power and grandeur."

Carter approached a statue and reached out to touch the solid stone. "This place must have had extreme historical significance based on the excellent craftsmanship." "I believe we're getting close."

"This hall feels like a beginning or an introduction to something major," Elara said, nodding.

Inscriptions at the bottoms of the sculptures came into play when Alice noticed them and alerted the team that they "spoke of guardianship, of protecting a valued secret."

Jade responded, approaching Alice, "I've run across such tales in my research. Lore speaks of a place where truths are both buried and revealed."

"We should proceed cautiously because we are not the first to attempt to learn the mysteries of the Manifesto," Ethan said, pointing to a far doorway that might be their entrance.

Maxwell remarked, lost in concentration, "And others before us, according to the accounts, never came out."

"We've had issues in the past. We shall prevail over this one, too," Serena said to uplift the group's spirits, "Let's move on but remain watchful."

The group cautiously approached the doorway with a shared objective in mind, ready to face whatever mysteries lay beyond.

Its broad wooden surface was covered in intricate patterns that shimmered as if they were alive with some otherworldly force, the designs echoing the team's common goal by referring to intertwined destinies, and excitement filled the air as they approached the door.

"This feels ancient and familiar, as if a power more significant than ourselves had sent us here," Serena thought as she hesitated and placed her palm just in front of the intricate door handle.

"We need a key or a phrase, Alice. This door won't open itself, destiny, or no destiny," Ethan nodded, his analytical mind constantly at work.

As Alice moved closer, her gaze fixed on the array of symbols, the patterns on the door illuminated brightly in response. At the same time, she mumbled phrases from a lost tongue with intense concentration.

Maxwell put the antique coin he found earlier in their trek into a concealed slot. The currency plus Alice's chanting set off a mechanism, opening the enormous door with a slow creak.

"The conclusion of our search, the secret we have been following, might be concealed beyond this door," Kofi said, his voice trembling with intensity as they entered.

Elara, the unwavering beacon of positivity, declared, "We'll face it together like we've done everything else."

"Each of our talents has brought us this far. We are not here by accident," Jade added, realizing the gravity of the circumstance.

"Let's find out what the sands have long kept hidden," Carter said, looking resolutely forward.

As they passed through the imposing entrance, a vast chamber unfolded before them, the air heavy with the scent of dusty paper and lost knowledge, the room surrounded by imposing stone pillars, the mosaic floor adorned with images of earlier civilizations.

His fingers traced the intricate patterns, finding sequences and practices. Ethan was the first to see something because of his keen vision. "They are not just works of art. They serve as a story and a manual."

Jade knelt to examine the stonework and said, "It's a map, and these symbols signify different epochs," pointing at a hieroglyph that resembled the one they had seen on the door. "See? This one portrays the rule of an obscure pharaoh."

Maxwell reasoned with his broad historical knowledge, "Every stone here speaks of a period when enormous powers moved beneath the earth and skies."

As she nodded in agreement, Alice said, "We're experiencing history, uncovering the mysteries layer by layer, and every step we take connects us more and more to the recesses of the past."

"You should see this, Elara, Carter, and Kofi since it could be our next clue," Serena said, gesturing toward the pedestal in the center that carried an ancient manuscript.

The room appeared to pulse with new energy as they looked at the ancient ink, inspiring them to continue searching. Carter, known for acting swiftly, carefully unfolded the scroll.

With a grimace, Alice leaned forward and stared at the script, her fingertips softly tracing the letters, a detailed depiction of the desert environment, complemented with symbols and statements written in a language unknown to most people. Despite being a combination of old languages, it has a structure and a pattern.

"We're looking at a journey," Kofi explained, pointing to a short red line that wound through the desert landscape, through secret cities, and finally came to rest at a pyramid structure. Kofi held up a small magnifying glass with care.

Jade shouted, "This could carry us to the center of the Manifesto, and this pyramid might be its last resting place."

"We must move fast since we aren't the only ones with this map right now, and our pursuers will be close behind." Elara contemplated their next course of action.

"Let's trust each other and the path forward," Serena said as she gripped her staff more firmly, and her determination could be seen in her eyes. "We are capable and knowledgeable. We overcame difficulties and are now stronger and united."

The Hades Manifesto's location weighed heavily on their shoulders. Still, they persisted, pushing further into history with each step. The group gave a collective nod as they began to plan, utilizing the variety of skills they had at their disposal.

The ancient travel routes were revealed as the sands beneath them changed with the wind. The group gathered their belongings and plotted their course for the pyramid with a newfound understanding of the journey ahead. Their movements were guided by Elara's shrewd intuition, which made sure they avoided dangers and traps.

"We walk in their footsteps, but our journey is different." Carter whispered, "This is what our forebears trod." as he felt the weight of history on his feet.

"We can maintain our course because I can track it," regardless of how faint it is. Maxwell's understanding of technology was used as he checked topographical information on the map with a handheld device and said, "There's a small frequency radiating from the pyramid."

"The desert hides many mysteries, but it's time we expose one of the largest," stated Jade as she took in her surroundings and the eternally golden horizon.

"We're reaching a place that's more than just an architectural marvel; it's a tribute to human will and a reminder of the legacies lost to time," Serena said as she felt the mood shift, and Ethan, who was ever watchful, examined their surroundings to make sure they were hidden from any potential enemies.

With each step they took, they could sense the pulse of an undiscovered legacy as they moved among the ruins of a bygone era.

Using her knowledge of the environment, Elara suggested that they walk in a zigzag pattern to conserve energy and avoid the desert's unreliable whims. The team labored harder to ascend the pyramid; the more sand they kicked up with each stride, the more complex their task got.

"We just need to learn to interpret the story that the sands are trying to tell us. We can't waste our strength," she warned, covering her face to protect it from the wind-borne dust.

"We are moving through a living history; each grain is a tribute to time, shaped over many years by wind and heat." Kofi nodded in agreement.

Alice's ability to decipher inscriptions revealed stories of a guardian ghost watching over the pyramid, which held promise and peril, on smaller, broken obelisks strewn across their path as artifacts from a former period.

Carter opened a compact pair of binoculars and examined the horizon as the group paused, ensuring that their route remained free of natural hazards and potential threats. His objective was to maintain the group's coordinated movements and push together. Jade prayed in silence to the spirits of the desert, feeling the weight of their task, asking them to be merciful. Serena and Ethan exchanged looks as they realized their difficulties had only begun. Maxwell tried digitally capturing Alice's translations as he stayed close to her. "This could help us inside," he said.

The pyramid's stones were carved with tales of time, victory, and the courage of those who dared to dream. They looked even more magnificent as the sun dipped low, casting elongated shadows, and bathing the desert in a golden tint.

They were suddenly surrounded by the pyramid, which had seemed so far away only hours earlier because of its vast size; it served as a startling reminder of the power and lasting impact of the ancient civilizations they were finding as the temperature dropped. The oppressive heat of the desert started to decrease.

"We are close," Elara said, placing a palm on the icy, sand-worn stone. "There is a pulse here, like an energy."

Alice replied, "We just need to listen," her linguistic interest awakened. "Every civilization has a heartbeat and a rhythm, which are the essence of their story."

Kofi said, eyes sparkling, "And we're the fortunate ones, getting to hear it after all these millennia."

The homemade torches produced disturbing shadows on the face of the pyramid. Jade and Ethan coordinated their communication devices, Maxwell set up his equipment for night vision, and the team stayed connected.

"We're here not just to recover the Hades Manifesto but to understand and appreciate the legacy of those who came before us," said Carter, gathering everyone. "Tomorrow, we go deeply into the history, and find all the secrets and understand the "Legacy of the Lost."

The remnants of a long-ago era were just waiting to be revealed and tangled with their fates, the group set up camp at the base of the pyramid as the stars started to appear in the vast desert sky, covering the area in a silver sheen.

Chapter Nine: Legacy of the Lost

As the team reached the pyramid's ancient corridors, the wind welcomed them with echoes of bygone eras. The darkness stirred up memories as Carter's flashlight's focused beam cut through the night. The ancient monarchs, their victories, their wars, their alliances, and their transgressions were depicted in the hieroglyphs. However, for Carter, some symbols recalled a hauntingly personal story. Little did he know that this mission would irrevocably change the trajectory of his life.

The dust particles caught in the torchlight whirled in captivating patterns as they walked deeper inside the pyramid. They briefly had the appearance of restless souls awakened from a long slumber, and their dance told a tale. Each step they took was a plunge into a time where the past and the present collided; the air seemed thick with reverence and melancholy.

Carter was under Alice's watchful eye as she was aware of his moods. His eyes were distant, and she recognized how his fingers periodically stroked the hieroglyphs. Her intuition made the connection: "This isn't your first time among these ruins, is it?" she thought aloud in a murmur, but Carter didn't respond; the emerging memories were evident in his eyes, reflecting the torchlight. There were numerous mysteries hidden in the pyramid's shadows, and the ancient, dusty walls witnessed quite a few; some of them had something to do with Carter's past.

The atmosphere grew denser the further they went, as though the winds had adopted a formidable pattern to them. Carter walked steadily, but his once confident strides were now shaky and started to stutter; he wondered if it was really the right thing to do, the right place to be. Elara's sharp senses detected an ancient, well-known odor. The mixture of burned paper and ash gave hints that it might be artifacts or documents from a long-ago trip. She halted and addressed Kofi, "Can you feel it? Something important happened here."

Kofi nodded as the pressure of his environment weighed heavily on him. He felt the walls closing in on him, though he was not claustrophobic. The complicated nature of their mission and Carter's past were beginning to be reflected in the pyramid's convoluted structure. Kofi's voice was barely audible as he replied, his eyes darting toward Carter. "I do. And I think it's profoundly related to Carter. He's been here before, and not just as an explorer."

Serena found a partially burned manuscript with singed borders and illegible writing. Maxwell watched Serena gently unfolding her excitement as a historian, making him look over her shoulder. Carter's face lost all color as he caught sight of the page, the wording barely readable, but one phrase stuck out - "The Hades Directive."

His voice was choked with passion as he mumbled, "This...this is the same mission I was on. The manifesto wasn't simply a myth; it was the cause of our demise, and it was the one that cost me everything." He started to pant lightly.

The group was shocked by the realization; they underestimated how high the stakes were. They exchanged concerned glances and figured they needed to locate the Manifesto but also ensure it wasn't doing the same kind of destruction it had in the past.

Ethereal shafts of light broke through the dimness, revealing additional remnants of the previous expedition as the dust was agitated by their movements. One was a worn-out silver emblem bearing the fearsome eagle holding a globe from Carter's former unit symbol. Alice carefully took it in her hands, her fingers gliding over the worn mark, and said, "Is this from your team, Carter?"

Carter nodded, pausing before responding. "We were tasked with securing the manifesto because we thought it would answer some geopolitical conundrums. However, we were duped; it turned out to be much more dangerous than we imagined. That badge belonged to my best friend, Alex, who was with me on the Hades Directive mission."

"Then what makes our enterprise different? If your elite force couldn't manage the manifesto, what chance do we stand? We're heading into the same trap, aren't we?" Jade remarked with a worried look on her face.

Carter's sad eyes came face to face with Jade's resolute ones. "The threat is known, and more importantly, we have each other. Back then, we were seeking glory, not recognizing the actual nature of our endeavor."

Elara cleared her throat and said, "History offers us a chance to learn, not repeat. Whatever occurred in the past, we're here together today. Our strength resides in unity and realizing the importance of our mission," after noticing the heaviness in the air.

The team's tenacity helped Carter with his past as he turned to gaze at them. But there were still unspoken tales and regret glimmering in his eyes.

Ethan chose to direct the conversation more strategically after taking note of the changing sands around them. "Our top priority, Carter, is locating a safe route across this region because sandstorms are unexpected and potentially fatal. Nevertheless, your prior experiences are invaluable." Ethan maintained eye contact with Carter for a while and then looked around at the group.

The historian Serena nodded and spoke, "The desert has taken countless lives over generations. Ancient caravans, armies, explorers—all pulled here by the promise of hidden riches or strategic advantages—all met their fate as a result of nature's wrath or man's deceit."

Carter rubbed his temples and inhaled deeply, bringing his attention back to the issue at hand. "I concur. Since it will get quite cold in the desert at night, finding shelter or an oasis should be our main goal." There was a moment of silence and then hushed whispers from everyone in the group. Amidst all the excitement and thrill, they had totally forgotten about the cold in the desert.

Kofi then took a parchment scroll out of his knapsack and unrolled it. "With my contacts' help, I obtained an old map that was supposed to show safe havens and routes utilized by the Bedouins. That could help us."

Maxwell bit his lip and said, "While this might be our ticket out, we shouldn't forget that the sands of time have a way of altering landscapes. What was once a route may now be an abyss," as the group clustered around the map.

"We hope this chart retains some truth in the constantly shifting dunes. Still, we must try," Alice said, nodding thoughtfully and drawing pathways with her finger. "We have to try, at least."

With her uncanny sense of direction, Elara took Kofi's map and scrutinized it, her eyes darting between the numerous lines and symbols. She pointed to a winding road marked with antiquated signs, "This path looks to lead to a sheltered location, an oasis, but it's perilous since it passes through the Valley of Whispers, as the locals call it." She frowned and handed the map to Alice.

Jade's ears perked up when the valley was mentioned, and her eyes widened. "I've heard stories about that location. It's said that the winds there convey the whispers of wandering souls, misguiding tourists. It's a disturbing and magnetic power that has captured many."

"Legends claim that those sounds are echoes from the past, from Carter's previous trip or even from earlier occasions," Serena nodded and continued, "They serve as a reminder of the price paid by those who disregarded the desert's power."

The recollections that threatened to overwhelm Carter caused him to tighten his jaw. "The job was supposed to be simple: get the manifesto and leave. But the valley tricked us into splitting up, and by the time the storm passed, half of my team had vanished." He had unknowingly clenched his fists as well. Kofi reassured him and touched him gently on his shoulder, "We won't let the past happen again because this time, Carter, we have the map, the knowledge, and most importantly, each other." Kofi's words offered little to no comfort to Carter, but he nodded anyway.

Even though the situation was quite serious, everyone seemed determined. The "Valley of Whispers" road was more than just a way to cross the desert; it was also a trip through the past, where they had to face old wounds and look for resolution. It was not an easy task.

The team made a makeshift camp as the sun rose to its highest point to escape the heat. Always prepared, Ethan carried a small, reflective-surfaced tent with him. Alice assisted him in securing the tent amid the ebb and flow of the shifting sands, saying, "This will help us prevent dehydration."

A water canteen was given to Carter by Alice as she took a seat next to him. She looked into his stormy eyes and said, "You've been distant since we saw that chart," she murmured softly. I hope you understand that it is not just the physical voyage but also the emotional one that requires preparation on our part."

After taking a sizable swallow of the water, Carter sighed and returned it. "I agree. We were so confident in our ability to succeed and our cause's righteousness. Still, the desert and the manifesto proved that they don't care about just reasons. I lost good people, Alice. Friends, family, and the like."

As she thought back on her own losses over the years, Alice's heart ached for him. She fought to retain tears in her eyes and not have a moment of weakness. "This mission is about more than just personal grudges; it's for the future of countless people. While I can't begin to fathom your emotional agony, I do know that we can't let the manifesto get into the wrong hands again."

"Carter, we're with you, no matter what lies ahead. We'll face it together," Maxwell said after overhearing their chat. He had joined Alice and Carter and seated himself near them.

It was clear: the group was cohesive. Their determination was the basis of their bond, and together, they would face the difficulties of the desert and their personal demons to protect the manifesto.

Serena approached Carter after silently observing the group's interactions from a distance. Her hair was loose, and the wind in the desert played with it, making it look like a golden net to block the sun's glare. She said, quietly but with underlying power, "You're not the only one with memories haunting them. The manifesto has touched countless lives in profound ways you cannot even fathom. There are people who have been affected other than you, Carter."

Unexpectedly, Carter turned to face her and observed a depth of comprehension he had never seen in Serena's eyes. He had never seen her so serious. His curiosity arose, and he inquired, "What's your tale, Serena?" He wanted to know her story.

After a moment of hesitation, she knelt next to him and drew her knees to her chest. She took a deep breath and began, "The power of the manifesto was known to my ancestors, who were the guardians of its secrets. However, one day, because of betrayal from the inside, its location was disclosed, and my entire village suffered. Before joining this mission, I had a life and a family."

"You were trying to restore your family's honor, which is why you were so anxious to find it," Jade interjected as she listened.

With her eyes closed, Serena nodded in agreement. She paused, looking straight at Carter, and said, "Carter, I understand your vendetta. But we must make decisions with our heads, not just our hearts. I need to make sure that the suffering and loss my family endured aren't in vain. Do you understand that?"

The burden of their shared history hung heavily in the air. Each of the members had a story of his own; still, it united them and urged them in their joint effort to defend the manifesto.

The campfire's lengthy shadows on the sands illuminated the features of the deep thinkers. Serena was one of them, and as she finished her account, Alice broke the awkward pause by saying, "The manifesto has a pull that I never realized. It's not simply a relic or piece of history; it's a binding force of our pasts and destinies."

Maxwell looked up from fiddling with some of the machinery and said, "It is stated that the use of power determines its character, but what if the very nature of power corrupts the person and causes them to seek more than they can manage?"

Ethan leaned forward, adopting a somber expression instead of his typically lighthearted one. "Do you recommend that we burn the manifesto? Is it a good idea?"

Maxwell reasoned, " I think yes. It might be the only way to ensure that it doesn't fall into the wrong hands. It is a good idea. "

Carter's hold on the driftwood he was holding became firmer. His facial expressions changed to a multitude of sentiments, finally settling on grief. He recalled the previous mission and how the manifesto had contributed to his enormous emotional loss. He pondered, the vengeance in his heart beginning to falter for the first time, "Destroying it would be the safest option." He spoke in a grave voice.

Kofi put his hand on Carter's shoulder to reassure him, "Knowledge will direct our path; we must first comprehend its roots and the extent of its power before making judgments."

Alice nodded in agreement, and so did the others. The team decided to dive further into its history, hoping to discover answers that would shed light on their future, considering their interwoven pasts and the lure of the manifesto.

Elara and Jade alternated, watching as the first rays of dawn appeared over the horizon. Perpetual movements and stirring from a tent indicated Carter could not sleep; given the circumstances, it was understandable. He was disturbed by flashbacks of that crucial mission, which suddenly reemerged with a greater significance, making them impossible for him to ignore.

Finally, Carter came out when he felt Elara's attention on him; the bags and dark circles under his eyes were a sign of the burden of his past. He said, "tracing a faded trace on his forearm, every scar, every wound I bore, is a sharp reminder of my purpose."

"You've never truly given the details of what happened. Only bits and pieces that seem too painful to relate entirely," Elara retorted and waited for him to respond.

He sighed and cast his gaze onto the horizon. "It wasn't only the physical toll. The manifesto promised so much—knowledge, power, the opportunity to transform our world—but all it brought in its aftermath was devastation for myself and the people I cared about."

"But understanding the manifesto's powers might be the key. We need to be sure of what it can achieve. Otherwise, we risk tragedy," Jade said after joining the conversation.

Conflict could be seen in Carter's eyes as he bowed his head. "We owe it to ourselves and those we lost to ensure this power doesn't cause trouble again, even if it's a risky route; you're right." He was fighting an inner battle, and he was tired of all the chaos within him.

Carter was given a cup by Kofi, who had been discreetly making tea over an improvised campfire. He muttered, "It might relieve your mind," understanding the suffering his friend was experiencing. He wished to help Carter erase those memories, but that was something he couldn't do, so he hoped tea would make a difference. Even a small one.

Carter welcomed the beverage with gratitude, allowing the steam to reach his face. His frantic nerves were momentarily calmed by the warmth of the beverage. Ethan and Serena were talking about the day's schedule and ensuring they were on track. Maxwell, ever the scholar, was trying to figure out how to decipher the manifesto's complex structure.

When Carter noticed this, he approached Maxwell and casually asked him, "What have you learned after having that thing for days?"

Maxwell raised his head, his glasses slightly misaligned. "The more I delve into it, the more I realize why your old mission was so important. This manifesto can either be a beacon of hope or a herald of doom. This isn't just a guidebook or some archaic guide. It's a living history, tracking the rise and fall of civilizations."

Alice was in listening range, so she decided to step in and join the conversation. "We must decide whether to use its power for good or to keep it locked up and concealed."

Carter stared at the ancient writing, the background of his grudge becoming increasingly apparent. "We determine its fate after we have fully understood it." His tone had a determination.

Luckily, the group discovered a secluded place beneath the overhang of a large rock formation as the daylight hours passed. In the meantime, Jade was patiently tending to a little wound on Ethan's arm while Elara was busy collecting some wild berries. They rarely experienced peace, so they made the most of it when they did.

During this brief and much-needed break in their quest, Kofi and Carter had a conversation. Kofi hesitantly asked, "You never really spoke about the former mission and how the manifesto played a part." It was meant to be a question and not a statement.

Carter plainly struggled with the recollections as he let out a deep breath. "It was a different time, Kofi. We were a team, much like this one. Our job was to steal the manifesto from a secure temple. Still, we underappreciated its guardians and the power of the manifesto itself."

Overhearing their discussion, Serena added, "It's like a magnet, isn't it? It lures people in with promises of tremendous power, but it's false. The manifesto doesn't offer power; it evaluates the integrity of those who seek it."

Alice came closer, her eyes displaying her interest. "So, Carter, just what happened?" She was excited to hear Carter's story.

But it was not easy for Carter to reflect on those times and the losses he had to endure. He paused; the agony and grief were evident in his eyes. "My younger sister was a part of that mission, and we obtained the manifesto, but at a severe personal cost."

The group held its breath as they could sense Carter's intense suffering. "You've never mentioned your sister before;" Maxwell eventually broke the tension. The experience Carter had faced was heavier than all the environmental pressure they had felt not so long ago.

Carter said, his voice trembling with emotion, "We were close. Lila was smart, fierce, and stubborn. She believed in the mission and thought the manifesto could be used for good and to benefit the world, but as we saw, its draw is strong. When the temple's guardians encircled us, she sought to utilize the manifesto and tap into its power. It backfired."

Elara extended her hand as a sign of sympathy and took Carter's. "Carter, I'm deeply sorry." Tears brimmed in the corner of her eyes. Carter continued with a heavy heart, "In the aftermath, the guardians reclaimed the manifesto, but not before it created devastation, and Lila was caught in the crossfire."

It's not only about the manifesto's physical strength, but Kofi also said solemnly. "It draws out the worst desires and fears of those who possess it, distorting them till they're unrecognizable."

"That day, I made a commitment to myself. To ensure that the manifesto never again falls into the wrong hands, to spare others from the tragedy Lila endured," Carter explained, his eyes gazing into space. He looked tired and defeated but not weak.

Alice had a challenging query. "So, Carter, what happens if we discover the manifesto? Do we trash it? Hide it away? Or what?"

"Destruction may seem like a simple solution, but it could be more complex. The manifesto is a conduit of power; destroying it might have unexpected implications that could be devastating," Carter paused after replying, as though the emotional wave of the memory had engulfed him entirely, and he was struggling hard to regain his composure.

Maxwell thought carefully as he rubbed his chin and said, "Maybe there's a way to nullify its strength without harming it."

Ethan thought for a while and then added, "If the manifesto is dark, there must be light," quoting an old mythology. "In some ancient manuscripts, there's mention of a counterforce - a balancing energy." It settled well with the rest of the group members.

Jade, who had been quiet for some time, appeared optimistic. She blurted out, "Are you claiming that there is another artifact, one that can negate the effects of the manifesto?"

"Exactly. If we can uncover it, we can ensure the manifesto's influence is restrained." Ethan nodded and replied.

Kofi asked in a cautious manner, "But won't it put a bigger target on our backs? Now, we'd be safeguarding not one, but two tremendously powerful artifacts."

"We don't necessarily need to keep them together. Separately, they're simply artifacts, but together, they're a disaster or salvation," Serena, who had been lost in her thoughts, piped in.

After learning of Carter's complicated past, the team had a renewed sense of purpose, which gave their objective a newfound significance. They were selected to secure the power balance that needed to be kept.

Suddenly, Elara pointed to a spot on the map that she had found earlier when looking at it. "The Temple of Lumara, known to be a sanctuary of light energy, could be an excellent place to start if we're looking for a counterforce."

"The Temple of Lumara? Isn't that where monks previously channeled pure energy for healing and protection? My grandmother told of it," Jade said with a perplexed expression.

Carter also recalled the name from a previous briefing. "It's deep within the Serpent's Ridge, a perilous road few dare to walk, and it's also supposed to be a spot where dark energies were repulsed and purged."

"Although treacherous," Kofi said, "It's also an excellent vintage point. From there, we can see any threats coming from miles away." He leaned over to get a better look at the map.

"We should split up. One team concentrating on getting the counter artifact from Lumara, the other ensuring the manifesto remains secure and hidden," Alice suggested with a bright smile. The heavy weight of Carter's tragic experience seemed to shift from her soul; she wanted to see a brighter picture.

"We're more adaptable that way and can respond to any unforeseen challenges faster," Maxwell said in agreement enthusiastically.

"There might be defensive barriers we need to get around in the temple." Still, Serena said I can use my understanding of ancient rituals to help.

"Temple of Lumara, it is," Maxwell said affirmatively.

They started preparing their approach to the Temple of Lumara with a nod from Carter. Every member played a crucial role in restoring the balance. The team's cohesion and complementary talents were their most useful defenses against the approaching darkness. The enemy was hidden and a lot stronger than they were, but their resolve was unshaken.

The Serpent's Ridge was intimidating not only because of its precarious routes and precipitous cliffs but also because of the stories of animals that lurked in the shadows and awaited unwary intruders. The group experienced an oppressive weight and an unsettling sense of being watched as they got closer to the foot of the Ridge. It was unusually dark, and their vision was struggling to grasp the objects near them. Despite that, Carter remained steadfast in his decision, thanks to his recollections of the mission that had cost him too much.

The wind seemed to pick up at Elara's comments, rustling the dry leaves and making the group's lamps flicker. She used her psychic abilities to say, "There are guardians here, old spirits bound to this place. They know our intention."

To the amazement of the team, the suffocating atmosphere lifted significantly, making the route ahead more apparent and visible. Jade, who deeply regarded nature and its spirits, gently said, "We come in peace and wish simply to restore balance. We mean no harm to this precious place."

Carter's memories became increasingly lucid as he walked down the Ridge. He thought back to a friend's laughter and the satisfaction of a job well done, only to have those memories eclipsed by the weight of the manifesto's curse. His heart sank in his chest as he carried his thoughts with him; they were attached to his mind, and as much as he tried, he could not let go of them.

Always on guard, Kofi abruptly gave the order for everyone to stop. "Wait, what is that?" He indicated a shadow that was hiding by using his hands. But instead of a beast or a monster, it was an elderly monk who was feeble but gave off a powerful force. The monk addressed the group, "You seek the Temple of Lumara," it was not a query.

"We do," said Carter humbly. "We need its strength to fight off the darkness that threatens to engulf all of civilization."

The monk took a moment to contemplate them before nodding. "Then, stick with me, and may the memory of the deceased lead you." It felt like the veil of darkness was lifted, and they could clearly view the route.

The Ridge's reputation as a problematic passage seemed to change as they followed the monk, turning into a journey of rediscovery and redemption. On the verge of a new beginning, the weight of the past was forward propelling Carter and his team.

Chapter Ten: Echoes of Deceit

The steady glare of the sun reflected off the golden dunes, giving the horizon an ethereal hue. At the same time, the immense desert's emptiness spread out before them inexorably. Their water supplies ran out as they sank deeper into the sweltering sands with each step. Carter was the one who initially noticed it; was it a mirage? But as they traveled, the hazy outline became more distinct, displaying the magnificent shape of an old fortress.

Even with the scars from the numerous conflicts of the past, its high walls stood firmly against the effects of time. Watchtowers in disrepair and faded banners revealed the existence of a once-impressive reinforcement that had weathered numerous sieges. The weight of the fortress's past pushed down on them increasingly as they drew nearer. This wasn't just an ordinary relic from the desert. It was rumored that the Fortress of Shadows, as legends called it, was where fact and fiction converged.

Elara started humming a gentle song as she became more aware of the spirits around her. She was speaking to the stronghold, pleading for understanding or permission. While this was happening, Alice glanced at the walls, her keen eyes catching glimpses of antiquated writings and symbols alluding to the numerous secrets inside. Kofi stopped, his head slightly cocked, as if hearing whispers from another world directing their course. Carter also assessed the layout of the castle to decide on the best course of action.

They experienced a powerful wave of awe, anticipation, and a tinge of doom as they approached the entrance. That this was a trial rather than merely an exploration became apparent. Even though they couldn't see them, the manifesto's guardians were surely keeping an eye on them.

Carter seized the initiative and pushed the hefty wooden gates open. Dust and sand fell from their hinges as they groaned under the weight of generations. Stepping inside revealed the size of the inside courtyard, a tranquil haven among the untamed desert. Old sculptures that each represented a guardian of legend could be found lining the walls, their eyes watching the group's every move. They were drawn closer by the enigmatic energy that surged through the fortress's center.

The road split into several corridors as the group moved deeper, each with its own allure. A third way was buried in darkness, with only the tiniest glimmer of light visible at its end. One path was illuminated by an ethereal blue glow, another by beautiful gold and silver patterns. Each path was intended to test one of them.

Elara walked toward the bright corridor, playing an intangible harp in the air with her fingers. In tune with the blue light, the song she started to sing produced echoes that pointed her in the right direction. The golden patterns on the floor of the neighboring corridor captured Alice's attention, and she started to translate the symbols after understanding they formed a puzzle that would test her linguistic prowess.

Kofi was lured to the shadows, inhaled deeply, and relied on his instincts to lead him through the gloom. His senses were sharper, and his steps were assured. While standing back, Carter tried to understand the architecture and identify potential threats. He understood the significance of each of their jobs. Still, he also understood that they needed to work together since the guardians of the manifesto were watching them and looking for any indication of weakness.

Carter observed the teams' movements through a central chamber full of mirrors, each reflecting a corridor's course as they traveled their itineraries. Elara's voice could be heard getting louder, channeling age-old songs that caused the fortress's walls to hum in response. Each note she struck appeared to unveil secret doors, remove obstacles, and unlock safe pathways.

Alice was close by, kneeling on the ground, and tracing the intricate designs with her fingertips while she mumbled interpretations. Her voice echoed the weight of their significance as she repeated words like "truth," "destiny," and "sacrifice." By deciphering the riddle, one could discover a mechanism, a path ahead, or a crucial component of the manifesto's puzzle.

Kofi relied on his instincts while moving along the dim passage, his enhanced senses picking up hints of the past. He was guided by faint voices that hinted about safe moves and warned him about dangers. His voyage was more about trust, an echo of past betrayals, and rekindled faith than it was about sight.

Carter experienced a chill as they continued. The guardians weren't just indifferent bystanders. They were actively controlling the difficulties, as evidenced by the fortress's environment's subtle changes, rising temperatures, shifting sands, and weird apparitions. Would the group be tested to the utmost by these trials? Carter understood the importance of their mission as the pressure of duty mounted, not only for the manifesto but also for each team member's salvation.

One mirror's reflection revealed to Carter that Kofi was pausing and painstakingly breathing. He was surrounded by hesitancy as though he were at the nexus of the past and present. A door before him was decorated with images of loyalty and treachery, which echoed his past.

Elara's song now had a melancholy undertone that echoed through the hallways. Each group member could feel the weight of her song, which reflected anguish and vulnerability while simultaneously igniting hope and motivation. With her voice, she was speaking to the quiet guardians of the stronghold and pleading for safe passage for her fellow soldiers.

In her area, Alice found a vast mosaic. The tiles showed a mythology about the Hades Manifesto that alluded to its history and abilities. Her translations became essential because knowing this story was necessary to the team's journey. She saw that her area of competence went beyond linguistics, including linking the past and present.

The team's resolve increased as difficulties became more difficult. From his vantage point, Carter planned every path to guarantee everyone's safety. He guided them with soothing accuracy, communicating with them through their earpieces.

However, there was a sense of impending dread. The fortress felt alive while appearing to be deserted. Numerous manifesto seekers, many of whom never made it out, had passed by its walls. Carter knew they had to maintain their vigilance, mainly because the guardians were watching their every move and looking for any indication of weakness.

A pool of water was reflected in the center of a large chamber amid the shimmering heat. Kofi moved in closer after being lured by a magnetic attraction. The water's surface rippled as he got closer, revealing bits and pieces of his past. Fragmented vignettes reenacted memories of friends lost, conflicts fought, and secrets buried deep.

Kofi has always served as the group's go-to source of intuition, helping them through difficult spiritual and metaphysical situations. But in this case, the pool managed to get past his defenses and expose him. Carter heard his friend in trouble and instantly called out to him, reassuring Kofi of the significance of the task. Kofi, though, kept walking toward the water while appearing to be in a daze.

Recognizing the potential risk, Alice attempted to comprehend any writings surrounding this enchanted water. She warned Kofi of its entrapping character in an urgent voice. But he appeared unreachable. The pool served as both a physical test and a chance to face one's regrets and doubts.

Elara tried to awaken Kofi from his reverie with a hearty and frantic tone in her tunes. Incorporating frequencies she had seldom employed, she echoed through the vast space with a resonance to balance the pool's might.

Carter developed a strategy simultaneously, including the knowledge of everyone. They had to remove Kofi from the pool and continue their mission while constantly being conscious of the attentive guardians. The actual test lay in surviving the fortress's hardships and helping one another when individual strengths failed.

A dark person dressed in the costume of the ancient desert nomads appeared from an adjacent passage amid the commotion of trying to rescue Kofi from the pool's hypnotic hold. This mysterious individual exuded an air of expertise and authority over the fortress's hidden mysteries. He was a frail, aged man with dominating eyes and lacked any weapons.

Alice, who has always served as the group's mediator, moved forward while scanning the tattoos on his arms. She tried to communicate, using snatches of the historical languages she had learned. As one of the remaining guardians of the Hades Manifesto's secrets, the ancient guardian responded kindly.

He explained to the group the purpose of the pool was to expose each intruder's deepest fears and regrets as a deterrence against those with bad intentions. Elara asked him for advice on how to help Kofi while plucking a muted chord. Her sincerity was noted by the guardian, who then started chanting along with her melodies to increase the force of the chant.

Elara continued talking to the guardian as Carter closely checked their surroundings to ensure they weren't stepping into another trap. Their conversation revealed more details about the Hades Manifesto, showing that it wasn't only a tool or weapon and a storehouse of knowledge that could be easily misinterpreted and abused.

They spoke in a way that suggested more difficulties lay ahead. The group prepared to explore more of the stronghold under the guardian's instruction, acutely aware that Kofi's ordeal was only the start of their difficulties.

The guardian brought the party into a spacious chamber lined with exquisite mosaics and ancient texts from a long-forgotten era. They were enticed to delve further into the meaning of each mosaic since it contained the essence of an old conundrum or tale.

With wide-eyed awe and a voracious appetite for knowledge, Alice instantly turned to one passage. With a mixture of fascination and caution in her voice, she started interpreting aloud. The paragraph described the symbiotic relationship between music and words, a potent constructive collaboration that, when used properly, could open the door to the next stage of their journey.

Elara was moved by the translation and played a hauntingly lovely tune that reverberated throughout the room. The old texts interacted with the music, giving off a faint glow. A section of the floor came apart as Elara's song climaxed, revealing a secret path underneath.

Carter permitted Kofi to take the point. He knew that Kofi's intuition would be their greatest strength in uncharted territory. The dimly lit passageway lined with torches appeared to go on forever. With each cautious stride, they made progress while carrying the weight of their goal. Each team member would undoubtedly be challenged by the unknown difficulties ahead. Still, they were determined to succeed since the stakes had never been more significant.

The secret entrance led into the core of the stronghold in the desert, where its walls gradually grew chilly and damp, suggesting the presence of underground water sources. They noticed markings engraved into the walls every few feet; these symbols were a secret language only Alice could understand.

The small passageway suddenly became a vast underground cavern illuminated in a gentle blue glow. A large underground lake served as the light's source. The lake's flawlessly motionless and clean surface revealed a cityscape that was submerged far below. Elara, moved by the eerie beauty, mumbled, "It's an echo of a civilization lost to time."

With his exceptional intuition, Kofi saw a movement below the surface. He gestured for the group to remain behind as he perceived a danger. Water sprouts appeared out of the lake as if on cue, congealing into fluid, shimmering water guardians. Realizing that these guardians would be another obstacle, the crew braced itself, putting their cohesion and resolve to the test.

Carter seized the initiative and quickly produced a plan. They had to escape this watery snare to learn the secrets of the Hades Manifesto and get one step closer to their aim. "Elara, use your melodies to quiet the waters, Alice, attempt deciphering any directions or instructions from the cavern walls."

Elara moved nearer, her resolute eyes glistening as she delicately touched the lyre's strings with her fingers. The cavern started to fill with waves of sound carried by a gentle, calming melody. The melodic frequencies caused ripples in the shapes of the water guardians, who had been prepared to attack. The lovely piece resonated throughout the cavern, sending memories of times when similar harmonies must have filled the space.

While doing this, Alice's fingers brushed over the etched runes as she drew frantically on the subterranean walls. She worked out a fragment of an ancient command that might disperse the guards by whispering translations to herself. She said, her voice barely audible above Elara's captivating music, "The water remembers. It longs to be reminded of the tranquility of those peaceful times."

Kofi, sensitive to the environment's energy, felt the undercurrents change. He felt a way forward, with Elara's melody and Alice's translations working together. He prodded Carter and gestured toward a previously obscured niche in the cavern that was now well-lit. As they approached, a stone pedestal rose from the ground, carrying inscriptions demanding the joint use of all their abilities. Carter started planning their next course of action as he sensed the weight of the difficulties still to come.

The inscriptions on the pedestal caught Carter's attention as he leaned over them. He immediately realized it was a riddle requiring logic and intuition to solve. The cavern guards became agitated as he reported his findings to the group and reminded them that time was necessary. Their brilliant shapes changed, their hues deepening to reflect their mounting agitation.

Elara continued singing, giving the music greater depth and rhythm to fend off the guardians. The guardians' watery bodies began to tremble due to the strength of her song, briefly causing them to hesitate and become perplexed. As she scanned the writings, Alice saw a grammatical pattern. This isn't just some random puzzle, she said. It conveys a tale that has been handed down through the ages.

Kofi closed his eyes and followed his instincts. He extended his hand and contacted a sign. It shone brightly at his touch and echoed Elara's lyre's song. The symbols started to brighten individually due to the team's united efforts. The water guardians reached peace due to the song's harmony and the resonance of the lighted symbols.

Carter muttered as the stone pedestal uncovered a concealed compartment, "We're on the right road," he said. An elaborate key with matching symbols was hidden within. He muttered as he put the key in his pocket, "This must unlock a road deeper within the stronghold." Even though they still had a long way to go in their quest to recover the Hades Manifesto, their resolve became more robust with each obstacle.

The team noticed a dramatic shift in the atmosphere as they were in the dim light of the cavern. Elara's music's soothing murmur grew dimmer as though muffled by a cloak of sadness. The guardians, who had earlier been unrelenting, have vanished into the distance, their shapes taking on an eerie gray hue as they watch silently. Kofi was lying in the middle, with a lone ghostly arrow penetrating his heart and emitting a menacing glow.

Alice's cry of shock was the one that initially shattered the oppressive quiet. With the pressure of the circumstance pressing down on her, Elara's fingers stopped moving on the lyre, and she started crying. Carter, who had always been a rock for the group, felt the ground quake beneath him. Their compass had always been Kofi's instincts, and his sixth sense had proven invaluable at numerous forks in the road. The light was now turned off.

They were on the verge of sorrow when a figure emerged from the darkness. Alice was there. "I've spent years learning languages, cracking codes, and understanding ancient tales. Kofi and I shared stories of our ancestors, of intuitions and guiding lights. I can tap into that to guide us as Kofi did. Kofi was more than our compass; he was our friend. But we must continue our quest; he would have wanted it."

The team's other members nodded their features a portrait of sorrow, grit, and optimism. Carter inhaled deeply and clutched the elaborate key, his eyes filled with purpose as he said, "For Kofi." They moved further into the desert fortress, with Alice filling Kofi's position, propelled by their sense and memory of their lost companion.

Without Kofi's comforting presence, the fortress's size seemed even more menacing. Only the sporadic sweet melody from Elara, intended to comfort the team's troubled hearts, broke the oppressive quiet that hung over them. Even as they continued to advance, the fortress walls' shadows appeared, whispering treachery, hidden secrets, and impending threats.

An impressive door with glyphs and archaic symbols was in front of them. Alice started deciphering while wearing a determined mask on her face. Her fingers brushed the chilly stone as she spoke, "These aren't just inscriptions. They convey a story that mirrors our journey—one of sacrifice and cooperation."

Drawing strength from their shared sorrow, the team discovered themselves forging a stronger relationship than ever before. Carter glanced around and said, "The guardians are watching, assessing us at every turn. We must employ Kofi's teachings and continue as one." Carter's tactical decisions were led by the rhythm created by the flawless blending of Elara's tunes and Alice's translations.

The door opened in response to Alice's final translation, exposing a different chamber with an aura of expectation. They knew this was only one of the numerous obstacles the guardians had put in place. However, Kofi's legacy continued with each step, driving them forward and ensuring they stayed unified in spirit and purpose.

The newly discovered chamber was a large area decorated with murals that showed scenes from a bygone era—when the stronghold was lively, the desert was lush, and its residents were at peace. Their senses were playing with echoes of joy and laughter. But that peace was offset by a menacing focal point: a vast stone plinth perched atop a complex crystal device.

Elara sensed an ethereal tug towards the object as they got closer. When the right note was played, it reverberated with her melodies and released its power. When Carter finished surveying the space, he asserted: "Alice, any insight from these murals?"

"This mechanism is the heart of the fortress, its secrets protected by the guardians' riddles."

While tracing the stories with her fingers, Alice nodded.

Then it dawned on her, "The crystal thrives on musical energy. It speaks of harmony and unity. Elara, you must sing the song of unity that overcomes grief and exudes hope."

Elara took a deep breath before starting her song. Each note shimmered in the air, fusing with memories of their journey—the difficulties they overcame and the losses they endured. With each chord, the crystal absorbed her singing and became brighter, erasing shadows and exposing previously hidden channels.

The team pushed forth as a unit, catapulted by shared beliefs, memories, and legacy, prepared to take on the difficulties ahead.

Three distinct rooms, each representing a member's talent, were reached via the passageways made visible by the crystal. Elara's route was radiant and shimmered to the gentle rhythm of her previous songs. Along Alice's path were inscriptions in antiquated languages that whispered legends from bygone centuries. Carter's route was a tricky maze of shifting sands and calculated difficulties.

"We must separate; the guardians want us to deal with things independently, but we'll reunite at the conclusion," Carter said, his gaze becoming more focused.

Elara paused and said, "Are we certain about splitting up at this time, especially after... Kofi?"

"Kofi would have wanted us to continue. To learn the truth he died protecting," Alice softly interrupted, her voice steely.

After sharing a solemn moment, everyone entered their individual domains while nodding in accord. Elara's journey tested the breadth and depth of her melodies, requiring her to produce sounds that embodied hope, anguish, and joy. Alice quickly solved puzzles and translated texts, revealing long-buried historical secrets. Carter, meanwhile, had to make calculated choices in a strategic simulation to beat the overwhelming odds.

Each participant sensed the guardians' pervasive stare, simultaneously assessing, judging, and softly assisting them as they dug deeper. Aware that the revelations ahead would fundamentally alter everything, they continued despite their quest's burden.

Each group member struggled with the limits of their abilities as the trials in the chambers grew more intense. Elara suddenly saw herself in a big theater where her melodies weren't just tunes but memories. She reflected on her life experiences with each note—some lovely, some painful. She developed her ability to compose songs of reconciliation in this echoing space, transforming her suffering into a melodic crescendo.

Alice, on the other hand, was faced with a monolithic slab covered in symbols and characters that were constantly changing. Lacking the time to decipher carefully, she relied on her natural ability to communicate through language, letting the words speak to her inner core. The slab synchronized with her natural language rhythm and let her realize that proper translation required comprehension and reading.

Every action in Carter's strategy room changed the environment around him in real-time, making it resemble a sandbox. Winds were channeled as routes while sand rose to create barriers. He soon realized that more than relying on strategy was needed. He would succeed, thanks to the constructive collaboration of his instinct, honed over the years on the field, and his analytical mind.

The guardians were waiting in a large central hall where their tribulations ended, their forms ageless and ethereal. The guardians started dancing a graceful waltz as the team came closer; the dance represented the passage of time and served as the prologue to Dawn's Desperate Dance. The team would discover their answers and face the realities of their journey here amidst beautiful movements and shimmering lights.

Chapter Eleven: Dawns Desperate Dance-

Their challenging way to the stronghold brought them to a difficult juncture, where the mysterious keepers of the Hades Manifesto were right on their faces. Apprehension and silence prevailed and was only sometimes disturbed by a gust of wind. The ground was holding its breath in anticipation of how this crucial encounter would turn out.

While grieving Kofi's passing, each team member found inspiration in his memory, which strengthened their commitment to their common goal. Elara stood up and sang; her voice was deep, creating chants and hymns that echoed the legendary tales of her people.

The guardians, prepared to fight at first, were mesmerized by this blending of music and chant. Their hardened expressions relaxed, and they gradually dropped their firearms. Elara's performance filled the gap of conflict.

An elderly guardian moved forward, his face having wrinkles and creases. He signaled a truce and said, "Your hearts and intentions are clean." He then turned his attention to the horizon, suggesting the last puzzling piece of their journey and the difficulty they still had to overcome.

The group experienced a truce, with the guardians, whose combined might with ancient knowledge, looked at the team with absolute respect. They had anticipated intruders looking for fame or dominance. Instead, they discovered spirits connected by fate and tied by Elara's tunes and Amina's peculiar chanting. The guardians' vision changed due to their combined musical energy, transforming enemies into partners.

Carter took advantage of the peace. "We have lost a lot and traveled great distances to discover the truths hidden inside the Hades Manifesto, so we seek comprehension, not conquest," he said, his voice echoing the wisdom of their journey.

"We've faced puzzles and challenges customized to our very souls," Alice continued, her fingers trembling, "But we stand here together, not for personal benefit, but to defend the knowledge from those who would misuse it."

The elderly protector gave a solemn nod. He started, his voice was heavy as he spoke, "The manifesto is not only a relic. To continue this path, you must prove that your aims align with the manifesto's spirit. It's a memorial to our past and a lighthouse for the future."

The group was motivated to move forward with unity as they prepared to take on this new task through the shared memories of Kofi, as they knew their friend would have wanted.

Amina joins the song. Elara motions for Amina to follow her to the front. The two women start a dance that exceeds time, and the guardians watch, interested. As the desert sands around them move, ancient patterns and symbols that point to the exact solutions they seek are revealed.

With his strong eye for detail, Ethan began to interpret the symbols and realized they represented a journey. He muttered, "It's a path leading to the heart of the manifesto's riddles."

The team, realizing the gravity of the situation, pulled together, drawing strength from each other and the memory of Kofi. Alice identified a word repeated within the dance's rhythm: "Seek unity in division, and division in unity." As they decided to follow this new course. The fortress looked even more intimidating when the early morning sun spread long shadows across the desert. Previously seen as enemies, the guardians now stood with a certain amount of respect for the team. Their commander, a tall woman named Seraphine, advanced with a grave understanding on her face. A discussion started after Elara and Amina's performance, as a team surfaced the cease-fire commenced. "Your goals are great," she said, "but the manifesto you're after has the potential to change our entire planet."

The group's strategist, Carter, seized the opportunity. "We strive to protect, not to exploit. We realize the hazards." He continued, "But we've also experienced the destruction caused by those who misuse it."

Alice's fingers were eager to decipher the symbols the dance had revealed. They were the key to realizing the manifesto's potential. Elara interrupted and said, "Our path has not been without loss, and our goal is pure. We seek understanding and hope to ensure the manifesto does not get into the wrong hands." Elara was still mesmerized by the relationship she had formed with Amina.

Despite her hesitation, Seraphine was won over by their honesty. She drew them in by pointing out the direction they should go. The next stage of their adventure was planned, bringing 'The Horizon's Secret' closer to them.

After Seraphine's whispered disclosure, the group went quiet. They would meet challenges on the mysterious path that lay ahead. An ancient map that was thought to depict the exact layout of their upcoming journey was inscribed onto the fortress walls, and Alice's perceptive eyes were drawn to it. Its intricate designs and symbols contained more meanings than simple geographic markers. Formerly the gatekeepers of these mysteries, the guardians were now their companions, assisting them toward comprehension.

Elara softly hummed a tune that was an imitation of the previous dance. It reminded them of their group's abilities and their discovered harmony. Amina drew a route on the map with her fingers, noting potential obstacles and safe havens, using her extensive knowledge of the desert as a guide.

A sudden sandstorm was brewing on the horizon as the group planned its course of action. Carter noticed it first. He shouted, "We need shelter," his voice was urgent. They could find safety in the stronghold, but they had to move quickly.

The thought of Kofi infiltrated the dissonance of action. His passing had served as an inspiration, and they moved forth with greater ferocity. Together, they strengthened the fortress's entrances to protect it from nature's wrath and prepared for the grueling journey's next part.

The team discovered themselves in an unexpected respite of peace inside the fortress as the sandstorm raged outside. They found relationships formed in the past comforting, and they thought back on the trip that brought them together. Amina started telling stories about desert spirits who had once guarded the declaration, drawing on the knowledge of her ancestors. There were earlier sentinels than the guardians. The dimly lit ancient map on the wall contained more information than just directions; it was a historical tapestry waiting to be revealed.

Alice approached the map with admiration since she had always been drawn to languages and the tales they contained. She tenderly stroked the symbols, joining the dots and revealing stories the desert had long kept close. "These symbols tell of the desert's heartbeat, its memories, and the souls it has cherished."

Elara began humming a protective tune after being moved by Alice's observations. Amina joined in with an old chant as her voice echoed across the stone hallways. Their voices worked as a unit to cast a spell that allowed the team to perceive the fortress's power.

Carter and Seraphine exchanged glances as a silent nod to the significance of the situation. Now that the dawn had broken, it was easier to see the way ahead thanks to the wisdom of ages past, the shared resolve of a dedicated team, and the first rays of sunlight.

The fortress's stone walls reverberated with Elara and Amina's music. The guardians were drawn out of concealment during this crucial time, it was electrified with anticipation. They emerged from the darkness covered in robes with ancient eyes that had seen many suns and moons.

Luna was the first to notice because of her acute perception. She muttered, her voice a mixture of awe and trepidation, "They're here." The guardians, formerly considered enemies, now appeared to be seasoned stewards of a legacy. Although their appearances were shrouded in mystery, their intentions seemed plain as they made a steady, deliberate approach.

Carter speculated, remembering his previous encounters with such beings, "It's not simply protection they seek, but comprehension."

Seraphine reached out her hand like an olive branch to the closest guardian. She said in a steady, serious voice, "We come with respect. The guardian's response was a simple head tilt with the tiniest glint in its ancient eyes.

The fusion of music and history built bridges across continents and civilizations, transforming what might have been a clash into an assembly with a common goal. The crew knew they were halfway through the dance, the remaining steps still unknown.

A guardian moved forward and removed its hood to expose a face that had been deeply engraved with time. Carter was the focus of eyes that contained millennia of knowledge. It asked, its voice booming with an otherworldly ring, "Why seek the manifesto?"

Carter fixed his focus on the guardian. "The manifesto contains facts for which the world may not be ready, but we believe it can also direct the future. We wish to preserve history, not exploit it."

Alice said, "We've seen the dangers of its power slipping into the wrong hands. We must ensure it's preserved." The gravity of their mission was made clear by the weight of Kofi's loss.

While scrutinizing each team member individually, the guardian was thinking about this. It then extended a hand, palm up, in a smooth motion. An ethereal projection appeared over it, displaying a disjointed map.

It said calmly, "The last component you seek is not here, but this will guide you."

The group exchanged looks as they understood their quest was far from ended. Their road appeared more evident after the guardian's acknowledgement. However, they faced a lot of obstacles.

Amina approached the guardian, her eyes fixed on the ethereal map.

She said, "These markings," remembering the symbols from the legends of the ancient desert she was told as a child. "They mention a sacred oasis that is only accessible to people with genuine purposes."

The guardian's eyes grew more intense. "Yes, the oasis is natural, and it is there where the quest's last chapter awaits, but beware—its secrets are guarded by difficulties that will put your group's togetherness to the test."

Alice appeared focused. Her team nodded in accord, united in their resolve. "We've come this far, faced inconceivable hazards, and lost dear friends. We won't turn back now. Whatever the obstacle, we'll confront it together."

Their faces were gently illuminated as the ethereal map started to shimmer. The guardian said, "Keep Kofi's memory close, for his spirit directs your route. The road will be revealed when dawn meets dusk at the horizon's edge."

Elara started to play her instrument, crafting a melody of optimism and tenacity. They were surrounded by a shield of protection as the entrancing notes and Amina's chants danced together. They were prepared to take on their most significant task since they knew it was coming.

Carter couldn't help but detect a hint of mistrust behind the harmony of Elara's tune and the rhythmic intonation of Amina's chants. He wasn't anxious because of the guardians or the impending difficulties; he was nervous because of Amina. He recalled Amina's brief exchange with a stranger days ago; the words were muffled and obviously covert.

His senses were sharper now that they were on the edge of fate. Carter observed and scrutinized every move Amina made and every private conversation she had with a teammate. He saw her stealthily take out a small thing and slyly tuck it away within her clothes as she bent down to touch the ground.

Carter grumbled, unable to express his fears aloud for fear of upsetting the harmony they had only recently restored. At the same time, Ethan muttered, "Trust issues? Once lost, trust is difficult to recover."

They would face one more challenge on their voyage. The group came together, their collective knowledge and expertise arming them against the incoming storm.

The guards stood upright, like statues from a bygone era, their expressions unreadable but their postures steadfast, while the gorgeous landscape shimmered. Elara's music reverberated, a moving melody echoing the difficulties they had faced on their voyage. Amina evoked ancient spirits through her desert chants, filling the air with a mysterious atmosphere.

On the other hand, Carter stayed on guard, his senses tingling with both amazement and suspicion. He kept looking over at Amina. While captivating, each mantra she sang sounded mysterious to him.

He observed her every move and noted how often she glanced at the tallest guardian, who had a distinguishing mark on his forehead. Carter had learned a hard lesson from his mistakes that sometimes, the people closest to you are the ones who keep secrets.

The guardians started to sway in a synchronized movement. They were mesmerized by the music and chants and moved with a grace that belied their intimidating statures. The sands began to shift as they danced, revealing a long-forgotten symbol carved deep below the desert floor, pointing to the last part of their mission.

Carter's worries about Amina's allegiances intensified throughout this discovery and unity, casting a shadow over the approaching daybreak.

The team and the guardians' shadows on the desert floor were made longer by the orange tint that was painted in the sky. Their interaction was more like a tapestry made of threads from various sources than a direct conflict or complete harmony. Elara sang about unity, tales from their native nations, and assurances of the future as her fingers played her instrument with accustomed ease. In contrast, Amina's hymns served as an appeal to the spirits of the dead, a request for wisdom, and a warning.

Carter's gut instincts grew more acute as the group learned more about their interactions with the guardians. He sensed a tug, an unsaid understanding between them every time Amina's voice reached a potent crescendo or her eyes locked with a guardian's. These legendary guardians were courting a part of Amina, winning her loyalty gradually but surely.

Amina never let her team down despite her relationship with the guardians. Her chants frequently evolved into alerts, and warning of invisible dangers. She was their beacon, guiding them through everything, including a sudden sandstorm and the undertow's hidden quicksand traps.

Carter was in a commotion as he struggled with his conflicting emotions. Was Amina's conflicted allegiance a problem or a benefit? Was she a link connecting two worlds, or was she balancing on a precarious tightrope? The group was aware that the solutions were waiting at the horizon's edge, where mysteries were just waiting to be revealed, as the last element of their mission came into view.

The music and chants ceased as the dry air whirled with strain. Together with Elara's music, Amina's eerie melodies created a flawless musical portrait of their journey and difficulties. Carter took a stride in the direction of Amina, his eyes penetrating hers as the last notes hung in the air. His voice had a trace of emotion as he addressed Amina, "Your link to the guardians—it goes deep, doesn't it?"

Amina paused for a moment, her eyes wandering to the guardian's keeping vigil. She said, "It's true. My ancestors were once linked to the guardians and chose to span the chasm between our realms," Amina said.

Elara played a soothing lullaby to encourage the team to pay attention and comprehend after realizing the seriousness of the situation. "But my heart and loyalties belong here, with all of you; my commitment to our cause is steadfast," Amina continued.

Carter nodded as the sun rose, illuminating the sands with golden hues. His confidence was reaffirmed, and the team's ties grew closer. Amina's discoveries made the way ahead appear more apparent, and the prospect of dawn led them toward what awaited beyond the horizon.

The ancient symbols on the guardians' foreheads shimmered as they stepped forward, moved by the team's demonstration of unity and their combined might. The lead guardian spoke to them in a voice that resounded throughout the ages. We can tell your objectives are sincere because of the strength and togetherness you have displayed.

After hesitating for a while, Carter took the initiative. "Will you help us find the last piece to accomplish our mission?"

Amina's heart beats in time with the rhythms of the desert. Her heritage ties her to us, but her loyalty to you remains steady. After staring at Amina for a long moment, the guardian said, "It was foretold that one of the lineages would return, and with them, hope would be reborn."

The guardian held out a map that was painstakingly crafted on an old piece of parchment. "The journey is just as important as the destination, and sometimes the horizons hide more than the eyes can see, so keep that in mind as you follow this map to find what you're looking for."

The words "Horizons Secret" hinted at the development of their journey. The group set out with the map in hand, united and determined, the early morning light casting long shadows as they continued deeper into the desolate area.

A dust storm threatened to obscure the path the guardian's map had illuminated just as the light appeared to have won the battle against the night. Amina chanted a desert song known to calm even the mightiest sandstorms as Elara played her flute in time to the rhythm of the approaching storm.

Carter kept a close eye on Amina. But the desert reacted when her voice mingled with Elara's music. The storm passed, the whirling sands settled, and the path they were meant to travel was once more made clear. Amina's position on the team was further solidified by this action; her dedication was undeniable.

Amina looked out over the immense space and said, "It's the Horizon's Secret. Only those who fully comprehend the desert's heart are given access to its tales."

They thought they were getting closer to the trip's high point with each step. They persisted, their connection more vital than ever, knowing that the end of this mission might just be the start of another as the last of the storm's remains disappeared into the distance. They had no idea that the mysteries they would unearth would pave the way for a hunt extending far beyond the desert's boundaries. "The Hunt for the Hades Manifesto" was merely the beginning of their quest.

Chapter Twelve: The Horizon's Secret

They faced a vast desert that seemed to go on forever and felt like a painting of sand and sunlight. The beginning of another day of hunting started with the orange and pink hues of the rising sun.

For a while, Carter, Elara, Amina, and the rest of the team remained still as they stared at the Cliffside of an old temple entrance. They thought about the rumor that the temple contained the truth of the Hades Manifesto, the burden of their quest weighed hard on their shoulders.

But this wasn't just any legend; it was the end of their difficult trip and the meeting place of fact, fiction, and myth. Carter took a deep breath, moved ahead, guiding the group to the temple's entrance. They were filled with suspense as they weren't just looking for an artifact but the truth that was guarded for so long.

The group felt more united than ever, with their goal now obvious. They realized that the Hades Manifesto represented more than just a physical object to be owned; it was a revelation, and an understanding of past, present, and future. The ancient gateway was a representation of the difficulties that lay ahead as well as the solutions. Beyond the doorway was the temple's heart and the core of their mission. Unbeknownst to them, a bigger foe was watching them as they dug deeper into the Horizon's mystery preparing themselves for a clash that would change their fates.

The temple's interior walls were covered in exquisite carvings that portrayed images from ancient rituals, conflicts, and cosmic alliances. It was fantastic but poorly illuminated. They moved farther into the holy area. Their voices and the rustling of the garments created a creepy soundscape, but they ignored it and went ahead anyway.

Elara, who was always aware of her surroundings, started humming a gentle tune that matched the temple's resounding frequency. As she moved forward, the dark passageways became visible and led the way for her. Amina was busy deciphering the symbols, establishing the environment of their voyage according to her extensive knowledge of ancient deserts. They weren't only in a temple but in a historical archive that had preserved the Hades Manifesto's historical accuracy.

There was also a complex maze in the temple. The team had to tackle puzzle after puzzle, and another appeared as soon as one was finished. It was tiring for them. They overcame obstacles uniting their strengths— but that wasn't always enough, so they had to use Carter's strategic thinking and Elara's musical intuition. Amina with her extensive understanding of the ancient desert, and Alice with her ability to understand and comprehend ancient languages, helped the group to move closer to the temple's core and uncover the manifesto's core truth.

However, a threatening presence became more pronounced with each victory. There was another frightening enemy waiting in the shadows for a chance to confront the group.

The atmosphere changed from calm to an almost tangible intensity as the team moved farther within the temple. It became electrified, much like right before a rainstorm. The group's historian, Julian, played the role within the group because of Kofi's tragic and sudden death. He took a moment to study a particularly complex fresco. The display of the stars was visible in the sky, yet one constellation caught his eye: a warrior standing with a bow pointed toward the Horizon. "The Horizon's Secret lies in this," Julian muttered, looking at the stars.

The same warrior constellation suddenly appeared above a large stone door in front of them. It seemed impossible, but Elara began to play a tune reminiscent of the warrior's stance after being inspired by the mural. Amina sang an old song detailing the warrior's voyage. The door started to tremble and reverberate to the tunes as its enormous weight shifted.

But as the door gave way, a lot of shadowy beings appeared and blocked their entrance. The guardians returned because they were responsible for preserving the truth. Our team prepared themselves with a common goal, knowledge, and abilities they had gained along the way. Although there was much tension in the air, it held the promise of the information they had been seeking so relentlessly.

Carter knew better than to underestimate the guardians because he had battled numerous enemies in the past. While fascinating, their presence was strong and gave a sense of extreme strength. The temperature dropped low, and the temple's walls were closing in on them. They were the last of the shields, the last hurdle the crew had to overcome to reveal the manifesto's truth, and their intimidating presence indicated as much.

Carter said with a firm yet respectful voice, "Stand down."

The guardians, who were all staring at Amina, did not move. Her connection to the guardians was clearer than ever. She moved forward and recited a passage from her desert chants that discussed harmony, understanding, and the perpetual cycle of life and death. Her voice was filled with deep emotions.

Elara's played a melody that matched Amina's words as her voice resounded. The guardians' posture softened due to their combined energy.

The group realized they needed to unite as they were making progress. Carter and Julian exchanged glances as they agreed that a goodwill gesture was necessary. They started talking with the guardians, creating music, and chants, seeking understanding rather than confrontation.

The reverberation of Amina's chants and Elara's songs combined to vibrate the walls of the ancient temple, producing a symphony that spanned ages. A profound silence filled the hall as the echoes subsided, highlighting the significance of the coming revelation. Sensing the team's sincerity, the guardians slowly moved aside to show a massive stone tablet etched with symbols that shone bright.

The team realized as they got closer that these were not just engravings but rather a living testament that was changing over time. Julian said, his fingers fluttering over the shimmering images, "It's not simply a relic of the past. It is a compass pointing towards the future."

Amina took a deep breath before deciphering the inscriptions, her voice was full of excitement.

She said, "These symbols tell a tale. It is a story of the universe's balance and the connectivity of all things. But there's also a caution, a test for those who understand its meaning."

The group began to understand their place in that epic story as they each processed the seriousness of the situation. The secret to the manifesto was not in having it but in keeping its truth.

Due to the frigid wind and stuffy air of the temple, it felt strange to all of them. The first to pull his weapon while scanning the surrounding darkness was Carter, who was always on guard. "This isn't the work of the guardians. Something else is here," muttered Elara after seeing the changing environment.

The distant corner of the chamber had a weak, flickering light. A ghostly silhouette began to take shape, its features still vague but glowing powerfully with wickedness. The temple's structure seemed to have come to life to fight the intruders.

Lukas, using his extensive knowledge of mysterious ceremonies, detected the approaching presence. It serves as a gatekeeper, a spectral being connected to this location, ensuring that the truth of the manifesto is protected from those who are unworthy.

Alice reacted quickly and made a protective barrier using her understanding of antiquated symbols. At the same time, Amina continued to chant in an ancient tongue to calm the spirit. Armed and ready for physical attack, Julian and Carter sat shoulder to shoulder. As the tension in the room increased, the group realized they were not only dealing with a ghost from the past but also the manifesto's anticipated difficulties.

The team could make out ancient engravings across the gatekeeper's threatening shape as it became more evident what it was. These inscriptions told stories of bravery, sacrifice, and the very truths they were looking for. The lines between the past and the present temporarily became hazy.

Amina said, "The manifesto is not a thing, but a living testament."

They understood the truth: their quest was not only about learning the tradition passed down but also about retrieving an artifact. It soon became apparent that they had to demonstrate the worthiness of this knowledge by fending off exterior threats and comprehending their own internal struggles and the cohesion of their relationship as a group.

Elara started to play her instrument in an almost trance-like condition, the calming tune blending with the surroundings. The gatekeeper's movements reminded Julian of an old dance routine, so he began to imitate them while flitting in and out of the music.

The gatekeeper started to respond to their combined efforts of human connection, music, and nature. Instead of a confrontation, a dialogue between souls began, one that would determine whether they were worthy of hearing the final truth of the Hades Manifesto.

They thought they were moving through a mirage as their environment seemed to expand and warp. They were no longer in the same reality as before, as demonstrated by an almost palpable environmental change.

The environment changed, presenting an old city that was a fusion of several centuries but was eternal in its splendor. The streets were bustling with activity, filled with individuals whose translucent shapes suggested they were not human. Despite visiting numerous worlds, Carter had never encountered a location like this. Its walls, streets, and air contained a lot of history.

A quiet voice said, "This is the crossroads of time."

The Guardian of the Horizon's hidden secrets stood out as the group turned to face him. "Every moment that has occurred and will ever occur is available here, but it is also protected. You must demonstrate that your goals are reasonable to access the truth of the manifesto—pure intentions must be for the greater good rather than just selfish benefit."

Amina took the initiative, understanding the guardians and their traditions, and said, "We are here to preserve the harmony between worlds and to better understand the nature of the cosmos, not for our own benefit."

The Guardian nodded. The cityscape shifted with a sweep of its arm, offering a lot of difficulties ahead. "Very well. Let your trials begin." They knew that to pass this test, they would need to combine their unique talents and have complete faith in one another.

As soon as Elara felt the repetitive pattern of the challenge, her fingers began to twitch automatically toward the strings of her lute. Shadows that resembled ancient warriors appeared at the edges of the city streets, their ethereal shapes threatening yet alluring. As they approached in a rhythmic dance of earlier fights, the air vibrated with tension.

As the warriors moved forward, the Guardian's voice resonated, "To know the past is to control the present." It wasn't only a physical fight but also a mental, intellectual, and historical conflict.

Carter made patterns in the air with his fingertips while reciting incantations to ward off the looming dangers. Each note Elara played on her flute was like a protection charm, keeping the warriors away. Amina, in the meantime, chanted mantras that appeared to resonate with the city itself, calling on its spirits for assistance.

Thanks to his excellent memory, Loukas identified the warrior shadows as representations of the historical figures. He declared, "They're not here to hurt us; they're here to teach us."

Loukas touched a shadow warrior.

The touch set off a flood of recollections, including tales of wars fought and lost and the birth and fall of civilizations. It soon became apparent that they had to understand, value, and honor the past to move forward. The key to the discovery of the horizon's secret was a more profound comprehension of history and its lessons. The team prepared themselves for a journey through time as they braced themselves.

Calmness descended across the place after the team's deep connection with the past. Elara's lute broke the stillness. The melodic strings played an old, sad, and hopeful tune influenced by the warriors' wisdom. The beautiful carvings on the temple walls shimmered in response as they resonated intimately with the building's design.

The ground beneath their feet seemed to hum in tune as Elara continued her eerie song. The temple floor's center eventually opened due to increasing vibrations, revealing a brilliant, hypnotic doorway. This wasn't just any gateway; it led to a place where souls were believed to be caught between life and death.

They understood the final piece of Horizon's Secret was not just knowledge of the past but also the difficulties of the present and future, with Elara's melody serving as the key. Magic and music had combined perfectly.

The group huddled close; their hearts heavy with understanding the purpose as they realized this voyage was just one part of a larger story. Their genuine quest was still far from over despite the difficulties they faced and the insights they encountered.

A familiar energy exploded from the temple's entrance's shadows as the group deliberated their ensuing action. The group instantly recognized the figure emerging into the light as one of the guardians. He was approaching in peace this time, evidenced by his posture and aura rather than an enemy's.

Always the first to move, Carter advanced while keeping his hand on his weapon, ready to defend his friends. But Elara signaled to him to stay back after detecting no malevolence in the guardian's actions. Amina began chanting subtly as she weaved a protective spell around them after realizing the importance of the situation.

"There is no need for that, Desert Whisperer; we are no longer adversaries," the Guardian said, as he took notice of Amina's song.

The only sound during the brief pause was Elara's flute, as it played a song that stood for alliance and unity.

"You're here to guide us, aren't you?" Alice asked, demonstrating her innate grasp of both Guardian and human emotions.

He nodded in agreement with their common objectives. "The manifesto was always supposed to bring together those with pure intent."

It was a striking understanding that former enemies might turn into allies. As they realized the Guardian's appearance signaled the start of a strengthened bond, the team experienced strength. Their shared mission was growing stronger and stronger, enabling them to overcome any obstacles that lay in their path.

They listened closely as the Guardian started speaking as they gathered around him. He told stories of worlds beyond their own, regions unspoiled by time and filled with people yearning for salvation, with a voice like the rustling of ancient scrolls. His descriptions of the enormous cosmos, where souls like Kofi were imprisoned in a never-ending cycle, gave rise to a striking mental image.

The Guardian said, "Beyond our earthly realm, there exist innumerable other planets, each with its own unique difficulties and entities. Some of these obstacles exceed the hardships you've experienced thus far," his eyes sparkling.

The team found itself enthralled by the Guardian's tales. Each account was a story of danger, excitement, and unmatched bravery. The stories took on an eerie depth thanks to the background melody of Elara's fingers plucking.

They were shown a vast, connected cosmos as he was speaking. It was a location where the delicate threads of destiny connected many universes. Once restricted to the hunt for the Hades Manifesto, their mission quickly grew. They were now searching for a cosmic balance that affected countless souls, not just one prophecy or person.

"This quest... It's not just about us anymore, is it?" Lukas wondered aloud.

The Guardian nodded.

The temple, which had before felt like a maze of difficulties, now reverberated with the wisdom the Guardian shared. The group had a reviving sense of purpose that brought them closer together than ever with each new piece of information they learned. It was no longer merely about finding an artifact.

Carter started organizing the data so that everything the Guardian said or hinted at would be remembered. Elara played a gentle melody that perfectly encapsulated their spiritual awakening. They had clarity thanks to this enlightenment based on cosmic stories and old truths.

"We're not just seekers of a manifesto. We're now the torchbearers of a profound truth. The Horizon's secret — it's not about reaching a destination but understanding the journey itself," Amara told the group.

Infinite experiences were promised by the Horizon's grandeur as Lukas looked outside. He echoed the Guardian, "The junction of fate and free will, that's our guiding philosophy now."

The group started to pack their stuff after being inspired by these insights and united by a common goal. The Horizon, with all its wonders, once more called as they prepared for fresh adventures.

They were unified in their objective and ready to dive into the depths of the galaxy awaiting them.

The enormous temple doors squeaked open, the vast desert awaited the group when they emerged from the murky passageways of ancient secrets, shining softly in the moonlight. In stark contrast to the heat, they had to contend with during their entrance, and the sand felt cool beneath their feet. Ancient tales were whispered by the soft wind as if the natural world were a guardian telling its history.

Amara took a brief break and looked up at the sky. The constellations aligned precisely, echoing the prophecy they had been searching for in an incredible celestial alignment. She said, "Look," directing their attention to a different constellation of stars. "Right there, as predicted by the ancient texts, is the mark of Kofi."

Lukas nodded and muttered, "Nature reaffirms the prophecy." The universe was on their side. Each star and planet intertwined to create patterns of hope, promising the return of their lost companion, Kofi. The night sky became their canvas of cosmic signs.

Carter noted the alignment as he anticipated it might be helpful as a reference. Elara hummed a tune, getting her ideas from the environment. The heavens had blessed their endeavor, giving them hope and newfound vitality.

The group was briefly awakened by Carter's comment, "The journey ahead won't be simple. But we'll find what we're looking for with the universe lighting the way."

The group set out with their spirits high and their hearts full of hope, bound by the conviction that their journey was illuminated by the stars and blessed by the sky.

The group stopped and stood shoulder to shoulder for a moment of contemplation. They had clearly reached the end of their search for the Hades Manifesto. They were now on a route to enlightenment thanks to the Manifesto, which was revealed as a truth rather than an item.

They were pausing together with the soft rustling of the desert dunes. Their imaginations were filled with images of their close friend Kofi. They could feel the wind around them and his wisdom, laughter, and unwavering spirit. Even though he was no longer there, his legacy was with them as he had been the center of their group.

Elara started playing a delicate, somber song that captured their sentiments of mourning and memory. Their loss of a hero they would never forget inspired her music, which became a homage and eulogy. The others joined in, blending their voices to create a hauntingly beautiful symphony.

Lukas moaned loudly as they finished their tribute. He continued, "We must go on. We stand stronger together, united in purpose, for Kofi, the Manifesto, and the challenges that lie ahead."

After that, the group continued, each step carrying the weight of their everyday experiences and the insightful truths they had discovered. They moved together in heart and spirit toward the Horizon, as it was called.